A Family of Foxes

A Family of Foxes

by

EILÍS DILLON

illustrated by

RICHARD KENNEDY

FABER AND FABER
24 Russell Square
London

First published in mcmlxiv
by Faber and Faber Limited
24 Russell Square London W.C.1
Second impression mcmlxv
Printed in Great Britain by
Latimer Trend & Co Ltd Plymouth

© Eilis Dillon
1964

I

Everyone on the island was talking about the foxes. It had begun with the fine spring weather and with the first sowing. The men sat in the cottage doorways in the sun, cutting the seed potatoes and instructing the children in the proper way to do it.

"An eye in every seed, like a one-eyed giant," said Seán Mór who was Patsy's father. "Take the knife in your hand now, and mind you don't leave yourself with no fingers."

Patsy cut, and four pieces fell into the seed-bucket.

"That's how to do it. Man, you'll be a champion."

Seán Mór called out to his neighbour, Mike Hernon, who was sitting on the creepie stool outside the door of his own cottage, just across the road.

"Mike, Mike! I have a champion here! Soon we won't have to do any work at all!"

"Next year we'll have a competition," Mike called back. "My two fine heroes against your Patsy and Peter's Colm—"

Patsy looked across at him sharply, to see if he were just making fun. Out in front of him, his two boys Michael and Séamus were sitting on their heels with their

heads bent over the bucket of seed potatoes, slowly and carefully carving with their knives. At the door of the next cottage, Colm was sitting with his father, at the same task. He lifted his head when he heard his name, and looked across at Patsy. Michael and Séamus turned around together. Suddenly Michael held up his potato.

"Look! It has a nose and a chin and two ears. It's like old Morty Quinn."

The others came running over.

" 'Tis the image of Old Morty, sure enough," said Colm. " 'Twould be a sin to cut up old Morty."

"That's no way to talk about your elders," said Peter, his father, though he had come over to look at the potato too. He stretched himself tall and pushed his fists as wide as possible apart. Then he said seriously: "When are ye planting, Seán?"

"To-morrow morning early, when we have the seed ready."

"I'll come before school," said Patsy.

"So will I, so will I," said the other three.

They all loved the spring sowing, when the sun had just warmed the surface of the earth so that it felt crumbly and clean under their bare feet. They loved the screeching of the seagulls that followed the sowers in flocks. It was the boys' job to see that the seagulls did not make off with the newly-planted potatoes. Sometimes they tried this, if they had not immediately spotted a worm. They were not easily beaten off then. They glared and shrieked as the old women did when they were quarrelling over trespassing dogs and hens laying out.

"When the planting is done, we'll have to get after the foxes," Peter said. "They're out of their knowledge this last year, nearly. Next thing we'll see them coming knocking at the doors asking to have the hen-houses opened for them."

Patsy felt a shiver run down his back at the mention of the foxes. As long as he could remember, they were always spoken of with hatred. Wicked foxes, thieving foxes, cruel foxes, stealing the widow's geese, breaking through the strongest fence, killing the chickens for the fun of it, long after they had had enough to eat, slithering off through the fields again with that high, clear bark that sounded so like a laugh. Patsy knew those laughing foxes well. Often he lay in bed shivering, wondering if one of them would come for him. Perhaps it might glance through the window and see him there in the light of the moon and say: "There's a fine big chicken!" Then it would come hopping through the window to take him away. He knew that was nonsense, of course. Still, the very mention of them was enough to send shivers down his spine.

In the evening, when the men all gathered into Seán Mór's house, the talk was of foxes again. Mike Hernon was there, and Peter, Colm's father, sitting in front of the huge turf fire pulling slowly on their pipes and filling the air with sweet blue smoke. Their legs were stretched out in front of them to ease their feet. Patsy, Colm, Michael and Séamus sat very quietly close together, on a bench against the wall. Nellie Seán Mór, who was Patsy's mother, sat on one hob knitting a wonderful new jersey that looked as if it would be ready for Easter Sunday.

On the other hob was Mr. Thornton. He was the teacher and so deserved extra respect. For this reason, Nellie Seán Mór had laid a cushion on the hob before inviting him to sit down.

"Sit down there, young fellow, and warm your shin-bones," she said to him, "and maybe out in the evening you'll be able to give us the benefit of your high knowledge and good advice."

Mr. Thornton smiled as he always did but Patsy knew that he would not give long lessons from the hob during the evening, as old Mr. Faherty used to do. Mr. Faherty was retired now and living in Galway. Patsy and the other boys had not been a bit sorry to see the back of him. It was like having school all day, winter and summer, as long as he was on the island. No sooner did he see a group of people gathered together than some demon got into him and he had to begin teaching them. The things he told them were interesting enough, but as Mike said:

"There's times when the rest of us would like to be discoursing a while too. Sure, he's following his vocation, but 'tis hard to be listening to the one voice the whole evening long."

The men had got very skilled at turning the conversation, asking each other questions, telling stories, to break the monotony of it. Nellie Seán Mór was always worried when this was going on. She was afraid it was not polite. She was so much accustomed to Mr. Faherty and his ways that she expected Mr. Thornton to be the same. Since his arrival in September, every evening that he came to visit she invited him in the same way to make himself at home. This evening he said:

"I haven't laid up enough wisdom yet to be able to give any of it away to my elders."

"Let you sit there, so, and maybe you'll have a chance to learn a few new things," she said.

"They say that foxes can turn themselves into men and women," said Seán Mór. "They say they are witches that get themselves up like animals so that they can move faster and live in holes in the ground."

"That's not Christian talk," said Nellie. "That's superstition. 'Tisn't Christian."

"My grandfather had that story, all the same," said Seán Mór. "They used to say the same about hares. They bring bad luck for sure. If I was to see a fox and I on my way down to the sea, I wouldn't take out my currach that day for Ireland free. I would not, faith."

"Neither would I," said Peter. "And if a man was to mention a fox to me on a morning when I was going fishing, I'd stop at home, so I would."

"Superstition," said Nellie.

"Well," Seán Mór said, "would you like to see me going out in a boat, and I after seeing a fox? Tell me that!"

"Sure, I wouldn't, and well you know it," she said, "but 'tis foolishness and superstition all the same."

"Foxes are powerful, for sure," said Peter. "The colour of them can bring misfortune, even. A red-haired woman is as bad to meet as a fox, my grandmother used to say."

"When do they turn into people?" Colm asked.

"After dark, when the children are all in bed," his father said. "Those are queer old stories and there's no sense in them. They say the same about seals, that they are really the sailors that were drowned at sea. They say that they come ashore at the full moon and change back into men, and sit in a ring on the sand singing queer old songs. And if you go up and speak to them when they're at this, you'll turn into a seal yourself and you'll have to swim away with them when the moon goes down."

" 'Tis because their heads are like a man's head," Seán Mór said. "Those are only old stories."

But they began to talk about pookas and fairies, half jokingly but with respect as well. Patsy knew that although his mother condemned superstition, still she always left a saucer of milk outside the door for the fairies on November night. And a queer thing was that in the morning the saucer was always empty.

12

"The cats got it," Patsy said to her once.

"Don't let the Good People hear you," she said. "They never like to be compared with cats and dogs."

"Maybe 'twas the foxes," Patsy said.

"It could be, agrá," his mother said. "They do business with the Good People anyway."

So every November night Patsy buried his head under the bedclothes completely. Somehow he did not want to see the fairies filling their tiny buckets out of the milk saucers, while a few grinning foxes stood by waiting to lick them clean.

The men were talking about foxes again.

"Every gun in the island we'll need," Seán Mór was saying, "and a few good dogs. The sheepdogs are useless —they're too much like foxes themselves, I suppose. But we'll have to bring them all the same. We must have enough dogs."

Now he seemed to have forgotten his superstition about the foxes.

"We'll hunt them towards the Fort," he said.

"They have burrows there in plenty," said Peter. "Only last week I was going up after sheep, and I saw one trotting along in front of me, and didn't he drop into a burrow so quickly I was sure I'd find the place easily. But I looked high up and low down and I could get no trace of it."

"Maybe he had shut the door after himself," said Mr. Thornton solemnly.

" 'Tis impossible to find the burrows in that place," said Peter, "because there's millions of holes there under the rocks. They say that long ago people fixed those holes to protect the Fort, so that anyone coming up the hill would catch his foot in the holes and break his leg."

"That was fine and handy for the foxes," Seán Mór said. "Only for there being so many burrows, we could block them all up and when the foxes would go running home to shelter, they wouldn't be able to get in."

In spite of his fears, Patsy could not help being glad that this was not possible.

"There was a man in Eochaill once and he trapped a fox," said Mike Hernon, "and didn't the fox pretend to be dead. The man was carrying him home by the tail, and his head hanging down over his shoulder. The fox bided his time until they were about half-ways home and then didn't he sink his teeth in the man's leg. Of course he let him go, with the fright, and the fox made off home to his wife and children."

"That's how they say 'as cute as a fox'," said Seán Mór.

After those few sunny days, it seemed that the winter had come back again. The sky was a heavy, dull grey and the white of the seagulls' wings showed up sharply against it as they wheeled and turned in the air above the potato fields. Now their voices were no longer cheerful. They gave a long, piercing wail with a whistle in the end of it, that was the lonesomest sound in the whole world. It was like a fierce wind that whistled through the holes in the stone walls. Huge white waves pounded on the shores of the island, day and night, filling the air with their roaring sound. No one thought of fishing, of course. The fox-hunt had to be put off. Everything had to wait until the storm would be over.

In the school one morning, Mr. Thornton said every-one was to write a story.

"It's to be a story about the island," he said. "All over

14

Ireland, in every school to-day the children are sitting down to write a story about their own place."

"How can we write about the island?" Tom Cooney asked. "Sure, nothing ever happens on the island, only fishing and planting and building houses. In Dublin, they could write fine stories."

"There is something happening everywhere," said Mr. Thornton. "In Dublin the boys are probably saying that nothing ever happens there and that if they lived on an island it would be more exciting. Open your eyes. Look around you. Think. Remember. The best of the stories will be sent to Dublin to be read and judged and we want a good story to come from the island."

"Can it be a story about pookas and fairies?" Colm asked.

Colm was only eight years old and he sounded frightened even as he said it.

"Of course it can," said Mr. Thornton.

"Can it be about cattle and horses, being sent into Galway on the steamer?" Michael asked.

"Of course it can."

"Or about a hayshed being blown away with the storm?' asked Séamus.

"Or a fox-hunt?" asked Patsy.

"Of course it can," said Mr. Thornton. "You see, there are plenty of things to write about. Now, all the morning you can think about it, and in the afternoon you can write it down."

By the afternoon, Patsy's story was fighting to get out of him. He knew exactly what it was to be. All of the boys had beautiful clean sheets of paper with a place at the top for their names.

"Good handwriting counts," said Mr. Thornton. "It's no use writing a story if no one is going to be able to read it."

For the whole afternoon there was no sound in the school except the whistle of the wind as it turned the corner outside, and the soft movement of the turf fire burning lower and lower. Only the older boys were there, because the very small ones never came to school in the afternoon.

Patsy's story grew and grew. It began with Father Fox, sitting by the fire mending a fishing-line and talking to his wife who was making a loaf of bread at the table. They talked of their hard life and how difficult it was to provide for their four children. The four little foxes were playing on the floor and the mother fox had to watch them all the time. If one slipped outside of the burrow, it might be trapped, or killed by a passing dog, or shot at.

After a while Father Fox got up and stretched himself, backwards first and then forwards. He brushed up the hearth neatly with the end of his tail and tidied away his fishing-line. Then he told Mother Fox that he was going out to get a bite of food for the family. A chicken would be good, Mother Fox said, and she needed some flour for bread. She gave him a little cloth bag to carry in his mouth and told him to fill it in some kitchen when the woman was gone to the well for water. The women always chatted at the well for a while, she said, so that was the best time.

Patsy wrote very fast but his story was only just finished in time. Father Fox was surprised filling his flour-bag, and he had to make off home with all the dogs of the island after him. He had to dodge around so many rocks and jump so many streams, and hide in so many clumps of bushes that by the time he got back to his den Patsy was hot and tired just from thinking about him.

Father Fox had broken the scent before he got home, by running through a stream, so that he was not followed right to his door. He was able therefore to go inside calmly enough, and he enjoyed putting off telling about his adventures until Mother Fox had begun to scold him for not bringing home the flour. She and the little foxes all agreed that they would far rather have Father Fox safely home than all the sacks of flour on the island. Then he promised them that he would catch a rabbit after dark, and that was the end of the story.

Patsy leaned back and read it all through again. He had become fond of Father Fox while he was writing about him. Now he found that he did not really want to part with his story and he was quite sorry when Mr. Thornton said:

"That's all. Be sure to write your name at the top. I'll be very careful of them. I'll read them all first, myself, and then I'll send them off to Dublin the next day that the Post Boat comes."

Patsy found that writing the story had made him very hungry. The others felt the same, and after they had helped to tidy the school and close it up safely against the storm, they hurried home for dinner.

All evening long, Patsy thought about Father Fox, and wondered how he was getting on in his den under the rocks, up by the Fort. When the men came in after supper they were restless and impatient.

"Such a waste of time," they said. "We can't fish. We

can't thatch. We can't plant. We can't even hunt the foxes."

Mr. Thornton was sitting on the hob again. He leaned over to Patsy and said very quietly:

"I read your story. That was a good story."

"When the storm dies down," said Seán Mór, "first we'll do a bit of fishing, then we'll finish the spring planting, and then we'll have the biggest fox-hunt ever seen on this island."

2

The next morning the wind had dropped a little. After breakfast, Patsy went to the door and looked away down to the sea. It was a greenish grey, the colour of a gander. All along the rocks the white spray foamed like soap-suds. Even from the door of the house he could hear the roar that the sea made as it came galloping in over the stones, rolling them around and dragging itself out again. Each time that a wave began to come in, the sound of its movement grew gradually until it filled the whole island with its thunder.

Patsy saw Séamus and Michael come to the door of their own house opposite. They leaned on the half-door together. They were so comfortable with each other that Patsy often wished he had a brother of his own age to be with always, as these two were. He said it to his mother once.

"And what do you want with a brother, and you having Michael and Séamus right across the road from you?" Nellie said. "Aren't they as good as any brother? And I'll tell you something: if they take after their father, they'll never change for the worse. There isn't a better man, nor a better friend in all Ireland than Mike Hernon."

It was true that Michael and Séamus were fine friends to have. They never started the day's business without telling Patsy what they were planning and asking him to join in with them. They did this now. Séamus called out:

" 'Tis not so black this morning. We were thinking of going down to the shore. We could get a few big round white stones for the path up to the school. Mr. Thornton was admiring ours yesterday and saying he'd like them above at the school."

"We might find a few glass balls too," Michael said. "Will you come?"

"Surely!"

Patsy turned back into the kitchen and said to his father:

"We were thinking of going to the shore and getting a few white stones for the school. Can I have the donkey and cart?"

"Saturday morning," said Seán Mór. "No school, and still ye want to go there with stones when ye don't have to go with books. 'Tis unnatural."

"Can I have the donkey?"

"Do, do. Take him out. He hasn't had a bit of exercise for a week. 'Twill do him good, the old blackguard."

Seán Mór always talked about his donkey as if he were the greatest scoundrel on the island, but he was really a very obliging donkey. Others that Patsy knew of, if they saw a boy approaching with the harness they lay down at once and rolled on the ground, or kept moving just a little beyond his reach, or walked through the gaps from one field to the next. They would keep this up for an hour before allowing themselves to be caught. Seán Mór's donkey did none of these mean things. It was true that he did not come trotting over to put his head in the collar, but he did stand with his head down so that Patsy could slip it over his ears. Then he lifted his head and moved first one ear and then the other, so that the collar lay comfortably.

The cart was lying there with its shafts resting on the ground. Holding the donkey firmly by the winkers, Patsy lifted one of the shafts, so that the whole cart came up. Then he backed the donkey in between the shafts, shouting at him fiercely:

"Hike! Hike!"

The donkey hiked, as he always did. By the time this was done, Michael and Séamus were standing by, watching Patsy at work. Séamus said:

"Do you think that donkey is deaf? Why do you shout at him so loudly?"

"I don't know," said Patsy. "Everyone shouts at donkeys."

"If I were that donkey, I wouldn't budge an inch for you," Séamus said. "I hate being shouted at."

"Perhaps he is deaf," said Michael.

"We'll find out, the next time I go to harness him," said Patsy. "I'll say to him: 'Please sir, would you mind backing a little more—just a little more?' That's how they talk in Galway. I heard them last summer when I went in to the fair."

They all helped to hitch up the traces. Then they got on to the cart, taking a corner each. Patsy had the reins, because it was his father's donkey. He jerked and the donkey moved out on to the road and headed down towards the sea. The wind was stronger out on the road, with tiny stinging raindrops.

At Colm's house, a few yards away, they pulled up.

Michael dropped off the back of the cart and went inside. A moment later he came out with Colm and they sprang on to the cart. As soon as he felt them settle, the donkey moved on again without having to be told.

Patsy loved the feeling of being high on the cart. There were no springs in it, and every time that the wheels passed over a stone it lurched and jerked. The wheels turning on their hard, ungreased axle made a rattle and a clatter that could be heard half a mile away. It carried even farther when the air was still. In summer the sound of the distant carts was like a strange, wild music. Today the wind whipped the deafening noise away with it at once, back and up over the ridge of the island.

When they reached the little pier, where the Post Boat tied up once a week if the weather was good, they turned to the left and followed a rough road along the top of the rocky shore. When the cart could not go any farther, they got down and wedged the wheels with stones. The donkey turned his head to watch this and held his ears pointed forwards,

"He does that when he's angry," Patsy said. "He knows he'll have to wait and he has no patience for waiting."

"It says in our book that the ass is a patient animal," said Colm.

"It's not all sense in the school-book," said Michael. "Even Mr. Thornton says you shouldn't believe every word you see in print."

"Our ass isn't a patient animal, anyway," said Patsy. "He looks as if he'd like to come with us. I suppose it is not very interesting for him, just standing there waiting, without another ass to talk to——"

"We could leave him Colm," said Séamus.

Colm looked dangerous at this suggestion. He said:

"He can stay by himself. Hasn't he a fine fur coat to keep him warm?"

But the wind was blowing up his fur in little tufts and they could see shivers running up his legs from the knees. They turned away and left him. He brayed after them wildly, with his big yellow teeth wide apart, but not one of them looked back, for fear of getting too sorry for him.

"I'll give him a hot potato from my dinner when we get home," Patsy said. "That's what he loves."

The top of the shore was covered with stones of all colours, worn smooth and round by the pounding of the waves. It was easy to pick out some white ones of an even size. As they found these, they carried them up to the road and made a heap of them, ready to be put on the cart just before going home. When they had piled up as much as the donkey would be able to carry, they went down below the line of stones to the big yellow sandy beach which ran from the pier to a reef of black rocks at the other end. The rocks were covered with sea-weed, blackened and bruised and rotting at this time of the year. This was the best place for finding the big glass balls that decorated the dressers in every house on the island.

The sea-weed squelched between their toes as they moved along by the edge of the reef. The tide was far out. It was the best time for finding the glass balls. Patsy said.

"They come in on the high tide, and they get stuck in the weed so that the sea can't carry them away again."

"I'm not so sure that I want to find them," said Colm. "I heard that there could be a little man inside in them, and he asking and lamenting to be let out. When you'd break the glass and let him out, wouldn't he grow until he was as big as the church, and then he'd eat you up in one bite."

"Bad manners," said Séamus. "How does he get into the glass ball in the first place?"

"He's put in there for his wickedness, by some good person, and he's to stay there till the Day of Judgment."

"If we see one with a little man in it," Michael said, with a wink at the others, "we'll keep clear of that one. 'Tis well to be warned."

"Don't mind those old stories," Patsy said, hating the look of fear on Colm's face. "My father told me that those glass balls are the floats from the Frenchmen's fishing-nets. They get free in the storm. That's all they are."

Colm flew into a rage at this.

"It was my Uncle Martin that told me that story," he said. "When I see him next, I'll tell him—I'll tell him—"

24

"Sure, he meant no harm," said Patsy. "Come on now, and we might find two glass balls, one for each side of the school door. Mr. Thornton would like that, I'm sure."

Colm came with him, but he muttered to himself for a long time about the little man inside the glass ball. They found two pale green ones. There were three kinds, pale green, dark green and white, but the pale green ones are the best, the colour of the sea on a clear spring day.

" 'Twas a good day's work," said Séamus.

They stood, Patsy holding one glass ball and Séamus the other, looking along the length of the reef towards the end where the sea broke white and foaming. It was then that they saw the two wet heads moving towards the shore, dipping under the waves and coming up again, slow and tired.

"What are they?" Séamus said in a whisper, almost as if he thought they would hear him and swim away again in fright.

"Are they seals?"

Seals hardly ever came so close, and in any case, these seemed to have long hair, Patsy said. They stood quite still. The two animals came on, rolling sometimes in the waves as if they had no more power to fight them.

"They're tired, tired," said Michael. "If they were seals they would be making for the rocks. Often I saw seals sitting up for a rest on those rocks. And seals wouldn't get so tired. They'd be at home in the sea."

"They're half-drowned already," Patsy said in a low voice. "We'd best be at the edge when they reach it."

They laid the glass balls carefully on the stones, and went down on to the sharp fine shingle at the edge of the low tide. Now that they were nearer, it almost seemed

that the animals were not swimming any more. They
made hardly any movement with their paws, but the incoming tide sent them in closer and closer with every
wave.

The boys walked into the sea until it washed against
their knees. The cold of it stung like fire, but they took
no notice of that. They stood in a line, a short distance
from each other, so that each pair of them would be able
to capture one of the animals. Standing near Patsy, Colm
said:

"What'll we do if they turn out to be lions?"

"They'll be too tired to eat us for a while," said Patsy.
"Now, come closer! Help me to hold him!"

Together they seized the animal and lifted it out of the water. Out of the corner of his eye, Patsy saw Michael and Séamus take the second one. Holding the heavy, wet body against his chest, Patsy said:

"We'll take them on to the grass. Don't put yours down on the sand, or he'll be covered in it at once."

He looked down at the bundle of fur in his arms, and saw a pair of tired, greyish eyes looking up at him. For an instant they seemed to cover with a film and then to clear again. Panic seized him.

"They're near their death," he said in a trembling voice. "They must be full of sea water."

At the top of the beach, they laid the two animals down on the rough grass. They made no attempt to move, but just lay there slackly, breathing jerkily so that their sides shivered. By pressing their ribs in and out the boys made them cough up the sea water that was in their lungs. Then they seemed to breathe more easily though they still lay without moving, except for their slender tongues coming in and out to lick the salt from their lips.

"Are they lions?" Colm asked, edging close to Patsy.

"They're the wrong colour for lions," said Patsy. "Lions are the colour of a red hen, and they're as tall as a man, if they stand on their hind legs."

"One of these on his hind legs would be as tall as me."

"They're not seals, anyway," said Michael. "Their noses are too sharp, and they have real feet, not flippers. I was wondering would they be sea-lions because I know those fellows have longer hair than seals."

"They're not any kind of sea animal," said Séamus with certainty. "Those feet were made for running. Look at their claws. And who'd want a tail like that in the sea? The weight of it nearly pulled them under, and the fur all soaked in the water. For the sea, you get a slippery tail like a fish, that won't hold the water."

"Maybe they're kangaroos," said Colm. "In our book at school, there's a picture of a kangaroo and he had a huge heavy tail at the back of him. The book says it keeps him steady when he jumps."

"But a kangaroo has a pocket in his stomach," Séamus said.

"There's no animal has a pocket," said Colm positively.

"Kangaroos have pockets," said Séamus, "That's in your book too. We had that book when we were in second class."

"Patsy," said Colm, turning his back on the other two, "you never tell me yarns. Is it true that kangaroos have pockets, like the pockets in my trousers?"

"Not just like your pockets," said Patsy. "They have one big pocket across the front, for carrying the small kangaroos in. At least I don't know if that's what they got it for, but that's what they use it for, anyhow. Why don't you know that, when it's in your book?"

"We're only doing the kangaroo since Thursday," said Colm. "We didn't get to the pocket yet."

"So they're not kangaroos, because they have no pockets." said Séamus. "And I'll tell you what they look like to me."

"What?"

"They look to me like foxes," said Séamus.

"But they can't be foxes," said Colm. "Foxes are red. We all know that. They're as red as—as lions."

"Look at their pointed ears," said Séamus. "Look at their pointed noses. Look at their long, thick fur. Look at their slanted, clever eyes."

"But foxes are red," said Patsy. "The colour of a red-haired woman, so that you can't go fishing if you meet a woman on the way with hair the colour of a fox."

"Look at their tails," said Séamus.

They all looked at their tails, which were beginning to dry a little in the wind and sun. They were speckled grey and black, with a black ring and then a white ring at the end of them. They were thick and bushy, and tapered off to a perfect point at the end.

"They're foxes' tails, for sure," said Patsy. "Even if they are the wrong colour, there's no animal in the world has a tail like that, only a fox."

They sat looking at them for a few minutes silently. Lying on their sides, they were stretched out as long as possible, with their necks stretched backwards.

"Dogs lie like that when they're tired," Colm said very softly. "Will they bite us when they are not tired any more?"

"No," Patsy said quickly. "They'll remember that we saved them from the sea."

"They look decent, quiet foxes," said Michael.

"They don't look like thieves and robbers to me," said Séamus.

"You can never tell a thief with his eyes shut," Patsy said. "We had a cat—that black one with the white front—and he'd rob the Bank of England if he got a chance, my mother said. As long as we had him, she couldn't put a thing out of her hand but he'd have it whipped on her. But to see him asleep, you'd think he was a real innocent."

"Do you think our foxes are robbers, so?" Colm asked sharply. "I don't care what you say, I'll never believe it." He stroked the nearest one to him on the top of its head as if it had been a dog. "They're not criminals and that's what I'll tell anyone that comes hunting them."

"It would take too long to tell, I'm thinking," Patsy said. "They're our foxes all right. Whoever finds a thing on the sea has a right to it ever after. But if the men see them, they'll hunt them for certain sure."

"Then we must put them where they won't be seen," said Colm. "That's what we must do."

3

For a few minutes the boys sat perfectly still, watching how the foxes' ribs went up and down slowly, with a little shiver in between. Their eyes were opening every moment and their ears were beginning to twitch.

"The salt water is tickling their skin," Patsy said.

At that moment the bigger fox sat up and began to lick himself like a dog.

"He'll have a thirst on him after all that salt," said Michael. "Wherever we bring him, there must be water handy."

"Wherever we bring them, there must be a stone floor," said Séamus. "Foxes are a fright to burrow."

They were silent again while they thought, trying to remember everything they had ever heard about the habits of foxes, and how to look after them. After a few minutes Colm said:

"I've been thinking hard, and I can say truly that I never in all my life heard a good word for a fox. All I ever heard was how to shoot them or trap them. They were telling a story in our house about a fox that saw the trap that was laid for him and didn't he drop a rock on to it to make it go off. Then he rolled on the ground and laughed and laughed, and went into his burrow. But the men had been watching and they laid two traps the next time. The fox dropped a stone into the first trap, but when he rolled on the ground and laughed, didn't he roll into the second trap so that it snapped and caught him. In all the stories it's the same thing—they always catch the fox in the end."

" 'Tis true," said Patsy. "We must hide them very well. I wish we could bring them to another island."

The others disagreed with this.

"Where would you bring them where they'd be safe? The men go hunting on all the islands."

"How could we bring them food on another island? We'd surely be seen, going and coming."

"Some days we couldn't go and come at all, if the weather was bad."

"Some days we wouldn't be allowed in the currachs."

"If they were on another island we'd never have a right chance to play with them," said Colm, who was stroking the smaller fox's head. "Think of it this way: where would the foxes like to be?"

"A wild place."

"A safe place."

"A dry place."

"A place where there would be no red foxes around," said Patsy. "If these are foxes, they are not like the red ones. The red ones mightn't like them, the way red cows don't like black and white cows. 'Twould be as bad if the red foxes were to kill them as if the men were to do it."

"The red foxes! Would they do that?"

"They have a bad reputation," Patsy said. "I wouldn't put it past them."

"A safe place will be hard to find," said Michael. "And we haven't much time to find it. As soon as they are rested, they'll likely get up and run off, and we'd have no chance in the world of catching them. Do you know that shelter for sheep, down by Casla?"

"The one that belongs to Morty Quinn?"

"Yes, yes, that's the one. Morty hasn't owned a sheep for years. He never goes down there. He told me himself that he's afraid of breaking his leg. Old people are queer—they do be all afraid of breaking their leg."

"I know the way in," said Séamus. "There's ferns as high as your head and brambles and thick, thick grass, all squeezed in between two little stone walls."

"That's the place. We'll have a job getting in there ourselves."

"We can walk along the tops of the walls. That's something old Morty couldn't do."

"Maybe if it's such a fine place for foxes, there will be a few red ones living there already."

They all shivered at the thought of the red ones, but they agreed that this would not stop them from going there.

By now, the smaller fox had begun to sit up too, and to lick herself in a tired way. The bigger one watched her with his ears cocked. For a moment, the boys wondered if he would allow himself to be lifted up, but he didn't struggle at all. He seemed to have got heavier since they laid him on the grass. Patsy and Colm took the bigger one between them, and Michael and Séamus took the smaller one.

"It's a pity we can't take them on the donkey-cart," Patsy said. "Even a piece of the way would be a help."

But this was impossible. The donkey-cart could only go on the road, and the only road ran right between the houses.

"I can imagine all the old ones coming out to the doors to watch us, and see what we have on the cart," Patsy said. "That wouldn't be a secret for long."

"Can't we take the ass without the cart?" said Colm.

This seemed a good idea at first sight, but when they came close to the donkey, carrying the foxes, he made it quite clear that he hated them. He pranced about and brayed and tossed his head in the air, backing the cart as hard as he could against the stones.

"It's queer how he doesn't like them," Colm said uneasily. "He'd never stand them lying across his back, that's certain."

" 'Tis the smell, I suppose," Michael said. "I can hardly stand it myself."

" 'Tis no worse than bad fish, or the shark that was washed up by the tide," Colm said indignantly.

"I could hardly stand them either," said Michael. "Come on, while we have time, we'd better shorten the road."

It was true that a strong smell, of a kind that they had never smelt before, came from the foxes. Since their fur had partly dried it had become more pungent, and as Michael said, only that a strong wind was blowing, they would never have been able to endure it.

"It's well they're not struggling," said Séamus. "This way we can go faster."

They went along the top of the shore, where the stones were round and smooth from the winter storms. With the extra weight of the foxes, their feet were soon tired and sore, and they had to sit down often and rest. Each

34

time that they did this, they were afraid that the moment the foxes would find themselves on the ground, they would spring up and run off. But they made no move. They just lay there quite slack and still.

"Perhaps they're sick," Colm said suddenly, and he began to cry. "Perhaps they're going to die. When we reach Morty Quinn's shed, perhaps we'll have only two dead foxes."

He hugged the one he was carrying. It put out a long, slow, pink tongue and licked his ear.

"Look at that!" said Patsy. "If that fellow was near his death, he'd never be bothered with licking your ear. Stop howling now, or you'll bring down the whole island on top of us."

Colm put his ear to the fox's mouth, to have it licked again. He stopped wailing, quite suddenly, and said:

"I know what's wrong with them, of course. They're hungry. We don't know how long they're in the water —it could be hours. It could even be a few days! That's what it is: they're hungry!"

And he began to rummage in his pocket with one hand, gripping his part of the fox with the other. He fished out a crust of bread, a bit grey but still quite good. Very gently he put it against the fox's mouth. The fox sniffed it once or twice, and then opened its mouth and snapped the whole piece, chewed it frantically and swallowed it. Then it began to push at Colm with its nose.

"That's it, of course," they all said, and they rummaged until they found crusts in their own pockets.

They divided them fairly between the two, but they could see that what they had was only like a crumb to them.

"Let's get them to the shelter first," Michael said after a minute. "That will give us time to think, at least."

They followed the line of the shore until they came to a long spur of land running out into the sea. Halfway along this spur was the shelter that belonged to Morty Quinn. It was no wonder that he no longer used it. The land was low here, and in winter-time the salt sea spray drifted over it, sometimes for weeks together if the sea was stormy. Now in the spring it would be quite a healthy place for the foxes, the boys thought. The grass was already long, because it had been a warm, sunny spring, and when they looked across at it from the shore, it looked green and fresh and bright.

The nearest house to the shelter was half a mile away. It was Mr. Thornton's house, which was a good thing because, being a stranger, he was not so much interested in the activities of his neighbours. When the island people were gossiping at their doors, Mr. Thornton preferred to be inside by the fire reading one of his books.

"Our foxes couldn't have a better neighbour," Patsy said.

The overgrown boreen led down from the main road to the shelter, but this time the boys came to it from the back. They climbed up from the shore over grassy hillocks all soggy with water and full of unexpected hollows. At the top, they stopped to look in every direction.

"No one in sight," said Séamus. " 'Tis like a miracle. Always when I don't want to be seen, that's the very time some busybody comes up out of the ground, you'd imagine, to ask me what I'm doing. If we're caught now, carrying two big black foxes, we'll be transported to Van Diemen's Land for certain sure."

"It's just as well there's no one around," said Michael. "We can't even stoop low, carrying these fellows."

They had to walk quite upright across the grass to the shelter. It was in a tiny walled field among grass-grown rocks. To the front of it there was a little cliff, not very high, and with a sheer drop to the sea. They could hear the quiet waves washing in and out down there. At the curved end of the spur there was the ruin of an old castle, very much battered by the seas and the winds. It was this castle that gave the place its name, Casla.

The shelter seemed a wreck, at first sight. None of them had ever been as near as this to it before. They stood in a row and looked at it. Then Patsy said:

"I didn't know it was as bad as that. The walls are good at least."

"The door is not so bad," said Séamus.

"There's more than half of a roof on it," said Michael.

"The floor is fairly clean," said Colm. "We can begin by sweeping it out."

The shelter had been built on a flat rock, which was worn smooth by the sharp little feet of the sheep that had been housed there. Colm and Patsy stayed with the foxes while Michael and Séamus broke off branches from the nearby furzebushes , to use as brooms.

"My arms are tired," Colm said. "I never knew there was that much weight in a fox."

"I was never near a fox before in all my life," said Patsy. He stroked the big fox, and then pulled its head on to his knee. "And I'll never again be afraid of foxes as long as I live, no matter what the people say."

"Neither will I," said Colm.

The floor of the shelter was covered with a sprinkle of

rotted straw from the thatched roof, which had fallen in some time during the winter. The boys brushed all of this outside. They found that the furze bushes made good brooms, and in a few minutes they had cleared the floor.

"They like a clean place, always, so I've heard," said Séamus when they had finished. " 'Tis always said of foxes that they keep their sleeping place clean and neat."

"There's a good word for them!" said Colm. "At long last someone has something good to say of them."

"I'm sure that some of the people would even put a bad twist on that," Patsy said.

The door was hanging by one hinge, but it was a good solid door. The second hinge was there but there were no screws.

"It's a fix," said Séamus. "What use is a hinge without screws?"

"What use would screws be, without a screwdriver?" Michael said. "We'll have to prop the door up with big stones. We're never short of stones, at least."

"It won't be enough," said Patsy. "Stones would hold it at one side, right enough, if the other side was firm. We can't have stones at both sides. When that big fox is rested and has his stomach full of food——"

"Full of food!" said Michael in despair.

"We'll have to think of that afterwards," Patsy said impatiently. "When he feels better, he'll maybe start hurling himself at the door, wanting to knock it down. We know how clever foxes are. He'll see at once how to do it."

"But we're going to tame these foxes," Colm said. "They won't want to leave us."

"That will take time. In the beginning they're sure to

be frightened. It will take them time to learn that we mean them no harm. They're wild by nature."

"So what will we do?" Séamus said. "I wish that we could just stay with them all night."

The others were silent, thinking of this. Then Michael said:

"I like our foxes fine. I'm sure they're better than most of the foxes that are going around. But I'm thinking that in the dark of the night-time, when I wouldn't be able to see them, I'd be remembering the old stories and expecting them to start up some villainy."

"So would I," said Patsy, "though I like our foxes too."

"I like them better than anything we ever had," said Colm, "and I don't believe they would ever hurt us."

"Anyway, it's no good thinking of staying with them," Séamus said. "That's only talk. If we don't come home for dinner, everyone will be out combing the island for us, not to mind what would happen if we stayed out all night."

Patsy said:

"We'll have to get a screwdriver."

"And some screws. Where?"

"Mr. Thornton is the nearest."

"If you start telling people about the foxes——"

"No, no. I won't tell him. He's the only man in the whole island that you can borrow a thing from and you don't have to reward him by telling him exactly what you are going to do with it. I heard my father saying that, only the other day."

" 'Tis true, he's not a bit curious," said Séamus. "Maybe it will be all right if he doesn't see which direction you come from."

41

Patsy left Colm and Séamus beginning to thatch the roof of the shelter with dry ferns and furze, while Michael sat between the two foxes with a hand on each.

"Much good that will do him, if they make up their minds to go," Patsy thought.

He ran along the top of the boreen wall, watching to balance himself perfectly. One false step and he would be down among the brambles and thistles. The wind tried its best to knock him over but though he swayed danger-ously several times, still he came safely at last out on to the main road.

Mr. Thornton's house was built with its back to the sea to shelter it from the wild south-west wind. When Patsy reached the door, he was quite sure he had not been seen walking on the wall on his way up from the shelter, because there was Mr. Thornton sitting by his kitchen fire, looking as if he had not moved for an hour.

He put down his book as soon as Patsy's shadow filled the doorway and said politely:

"Come in, Patsy. I'm very glad to see you."

Patsy came in and sat on the hob facing Mr. Thornton. For a few minutes they talked about the weather, and how the herring were running, and about the big English trawler that had almost been wrecked off the lighthouse island in the last storm. Patsy was longing to ask for the screws and the screwdriver, but he knew that it would have been very rude to start with these.

Mr. Thornton showed him his book, which was about a king named Odysseus who sailed on dangerous voyages in the long-ago times.

"I promised your father to tell all about him this even-ing up at your house," he said. "Would you like some

42

bread and butter and jam? It's over there on the dresser. I'll have some too, while you're getting your own."

While he was cutting the bread Patsy asked about the screwdriver and the screws.

"Take what you want," Mr. Thornton said. "The tool box is in the press there beside you."

Patsy opened the press and found a box with every kind of tool. He took a screwdriver and some screws that looked as if they would fit the big hinge of the shelter door. He sat for a few minutes more with Mr. Thornton while they ate the bread and jam. Then he said good-bye politely and went out of the house as if he were in no hurry. But once he had rounded the corner of it, he began to run as if the pooka were after him, back to where he had left the others.

4

On the wall, on his way back to the shelter, Patsy stopped suddenly to listen. The air was full of different sounds, all clear and distinct because of the fine sunny weather. The birds were twittering, not the full, round whistle that they gave in wet weather, but a shorter kind of song that almost sounded as if they were pausing in their work to whistle absent-mindedly for a moment. It was strange how they always had a longer, clearer melody before rain, he thought. The wind was singing too, strong and steady as it often was on a sunny day. It sang through the gaps in the stone walls, and against the corners of the rocks, and through the dry ferns and brambles in the boreen below him. A wonderful, fresh smell came from down there too. It was the smell of life and things growing.

"I'd swear there's a stream down there among the brambles," Patsy thought to himself.

With all the other sounds, he had heard a gentle, quiet bubbling like little voices whispering. It was not easy to separate it from the other sounds. It almost hurt his ears to try it.

"There's a stream for certain sure, and it's just what we need."

He sat down on the wall and leaned downwards, pressing aside the tangled brambles. They pricked his hands so that blood came out, but he hardly noticed. Here was the answer to their biggest problem, if there were really a stream. He could see nothing, but he heard it more clearly now.

"Where does it come from?" he wondered. "If it were flowing towards the shelter, I'd have seen it when I came to the end of the boreen."

Then he remembered that a stream ran in front of Mr. Thornton's door, that there was a big flagstone as a bridge across it. This must surely mean that the stream was flowing from the direction of the shelter.

"There's a spring somewhere under the brambles, for certain sure."

He turned and ran back towards the shelter. The foxes looked up when they heard him, but they had made no attempt to run away, Michael said. He had a firm hand on the scruff of each, just in case.

Colm called down from the roof:

"You were a long time getting the screwdriver. Have you got it?"

"Yes, yes. I had to eat bread and jam with Mr. Thornton, not to look as if I was in a hurry."

"I wish I had gone on that message," said Séamus. "Are the screws the right size?"

"Fine. How is it up there?"

"The rafters are good and there's plenty of little crosspieces to hold the furze. 'Twill be as dry as a house. I wish I had more practice in the thatching."

Séamus and Michael's father, Mike Hernon, was a celebrated thatcher. The boys had helped him a few times, but they had been allowed to do only a little.

"It's men's work," Mike said. "Wait till you're fourteen or fifteen. Then you can really learn the trade of it right."

Still, they knew something of it, and they were using the furze first and the dry ferns then, to make a tight roof.

"There's a stream," Patsy said. "I heard it."

"A stream? Where?"

"In the boreen. I heard it under the brambles."

"Fix the door quickly then, and we'll put these fellows inside," said Michael. "It's as bad as if I was tied to the ground, the way I'm holding them. Fix the door and we can all look for the stream."

While they were working at it, he kept on telling them to hurry, hurry, hurry, and asking why it took so long to fix a simple hinge to a door. At last Patsy said:

"You're making the foxes nervous. Look at them. They can feel your mind fidgeting. The stream won't run away. We can't go any faster than we're doing because we're just not big enough to hold this door steady."

It was true that they found the screwing on of the door even harder than the thatching. Each time they had the hinge in position and were just about to fit in the screws, the whole door would shift a little and they would have to start arranging it again. When this had happened a few times Patsy said:

"That door is laughing at us. If it does it once again, I'll give it a kick that it won't forget in a hurry."

The next time that they put the door in place, it did not move. Patsy put in the screws one by one and screwed them up tightly. The others looked at him with great respect. Séamus said:

"You're a useful fellow to have in a party like this."

"Nothing else would stop it," Patsy said. "Now it's fixed at last. They must have something dry to lie on."

"More ferns," said Colm. "Our cow sleeps on ferns."

"What do you think ours sleep on? A feather-bed?" Séamus said.

Colm looked as if he would fly at him.

"No fighting! The foxes would be off in a flash," Patsy said. "Ferns are the best though I wouldn't like to sleep on them myself. Once I lay on green ferns and when I got up again I was covered with ticks."

47

"Foxes are used to ticks," Séamus said. "They'd be lonely without them."

"Well, get the ferns, then."

Michael seemed at the end of his patience. They hurried to break off armfuls of ferns and lay them on the floor of the shelter, in towards the back. The stems were tough and hard to break, and this made the work slow. Still, they brought enough to cover the floor. After a few days of swimming, Colm said, the foxes would need a comfortable sleep.

They went into the shelter willingly enough, when their bedding was ready. The boys were pleased with this, for they had all been wondering whether the foxes would have preferred a burrow. They trampled down the ferns, walked around and around like dogs, pressing them down and sometimes arranging them more to their liking with a careful paw. They went gradually lower and lower until they were lying curled up, and then they wrapped their long bushy tails around them until the tip just touched their noses. The smaller fox had placed herself so

that she could lean against the bigger fox, using him as a pillow.

"It makes me sleepy to look at him," said Patsy. "It's a good thing that they like it in here. I wonder how long will they sleep?"

"Hours and hours and hours, by the look of them."

"They'll wake up hungry."

"And thirsty."

"The stream. We'll find the stream first."

They came out of the shelter and hasped the door shut, tying it with a piece of string from Patsy's pocket. Colm said:

"What will we do if someone comes here and sees the shelter newly thatched and the door rightly fixed?"

"No one will come. They'll all be busy. And if they do come, they might think that Morty Quinn had repaired it himself."

"What will we do if it's Morty that comes?"

"We'll think of something," Patsy said. "We can only do the best we can. Morty is so cross that everyone is afraid to walk his land, and he is really too old to come here himself. The last time I saw him, he had a hand on his back holding himself up. He had a stick out in front of him like a third leg and if it wasn't for the stick he'd have fallen out on his nose. He can't see very well at the best of times. And it's too cold for him to come from his house at this time of the year, even if the road was good. Morty will stop at home, you'll see."

He led them along the top of the wall, to the place where he had heard the stream come bubbling out of the ground. They listened, and it seemed to Patsy that the voice of the earth spoke to them out of the spring. He was certain that it was there. With all his heart he wished that he had tall fishing boots like the ones his father wore. Then he would just step down among the brambles and trample them flat, and push them to right and left of him until he would uncover the spring.

"We must get sticks," Michael said, "to push away the brambles. Bare feet are no good for this kind of thing."

But there was nothing near them except the thorny furze, and this was what they had to use in the end. Between the thorns on the brambles and the thorns on the furze, very soon their hands were prickled and stinging all over. Colm looked down at his with tears in his eyes and said:

"For those foxes, it's well worth it. I don't mind a bit."

They pressed the brambles aside as well as they could and then they had to climb down among them. It seemed that the thorns were everywhere, even in the pale green, soft-looking places under the branches. No one complained, because within a few minutes they had uncovered the source of the stream.

It must have been used for drawing water to nearby houses once, because someone had put a flagstone to cover it partly, and the sides had been neatly paved with stones. The bottom of the well was fine, silvery sand. Now that the sun could get at it, the water gleamed in little golden spirals and the sand sparkled and shone as the springs moved it gently about.

" 'Twas a well, for sure," Patsy said, and he laughed. "I knew I heard it. You can't mistake the sound of a spring well. Maybe the people from Mr. Thornton's house used to come here long ago, before the boreen got grown with brambles."

"Maybe old Morty stopped them from coming. 'Tis like what he'd do, and the boreen belongs to him."

"It's a pity the stream is flowing out to the road," said Colm. "If it was going the other way, we could be sure the foxes would always have enough to drink."

"Maybe we'll send it the other way, for a change."

Patsy had had this idea in his head from the moment when he had first heard the stream. It would take time to do it, of course.

"We must bring something to carry water in," said Michael. "Our hens have two dishes. I'll make off with one of them and it will never be missed."

"We got a new bucket for feeding the calves last week," said Colm, "I'll ask for the old one——"

"No, no! Don't do that! Everyone will want to know what you want it for!"

"All right, all right. I'll wait and see where it's put and then I'll make off with it. But I don't like that kind of thing," said Colm fiercely.

"It's for the foxes."

"Well, if it's for the foxes. But we'll have to be sure only to take things that are not wanted."

Silently they climbed on to the wall again and came back to the shelter. Food would be the most difficult of all, as they knew well, and it was no use putting off thinking of it any longer.

Outside the shelter they sat on the ground and looked at each other. Patsy said:

"What do foxes like to eat?"

"Chickens," said Colm at once.

"They'll have to learn to do without them," Patsy said. "Mr Thornton says that there are people in the world who never eat meat. If there are, there can be foxes in the world who never eat chickens."

"I suppose if someone's family has a chicken for dinner, we could bring them the bones," said Michael. "Or even a leg or a wing, or whatever we're given of it ourselves."

"We could do that, surely. And we could get lamb more easily. My mother is always giving me too much lamb, to make me grow big, she says," said Colm. "What about bacon? We have bacon very often."

"So do we," said all the others.

"We'd better not give them bacon until we have plenty of water for them. Bacon makes you very thirsty."

"It makes me hungry now, to think of it," said Séamus. "We'll have to get clever at slipping bits into our pockets."

"A leg of chicken, a small bit of lamb or bacon—that won't fill two big foxes," said Patsy. "We'll have to think of other things."

"Indian meal porridge wouldn't be bad," said Michael. "It would fill them up. And ordinary porridge and potatoes. Potatoes would be the easiest of all. No one misses a few potatoes from the end of a pit, and they're powerful feeding when you're hungry."

"We'd have to cook the potatoes for them——"

"No, no," said Colm. "When the dinner is over in our house, my mother puts the potatoes that are left into the big wooden tub for the pigs. I'll be able to get some of them every day, especially if I bring the buckets of feed out to the pigs myself——"

"I'll do the same," said the others, and Patsy said:

"We're all going to be very fond of the pigs for the next while. Everyone will be delighted with us. And I have another idea. You know how every time you go into any house on the island, the woman of the house gives you a slice of bread and butter, or jam?"

"Yes, yes, they do that always."

"Well, we can keep that bread for the foxes. Any time we run short of food for them, we'll just make a round of visits——"

"Sometimes they watch you eating it," said Colm.

"I've thought of that, "said Patsy, "and I'll tell you what you'll do. You go to the house and you sit by the fire, or on the bench inside the door. You'll talk to the woman for a bit and if she's slow offering you a bite, you tell her you're just going now and you ask her if you can do any messages for her. That always makes her go over and cut some bread for you. Then you just thank her for it and go out, nibbling the end of the slice. She won't know you don't eat the whole of it."

"If she's quick at offering you a bite?"

"Then you'll have to eat it, though you'll maybe be able to slip some of it into your pocket. Some women are a fright for watching you eat, and you can't deceive them if they're like that. If the foxes get half of what four of us get on a round, they won't be doing too badly. If we're really short of food for them, we can light a fire here and boil a few potatoes. If anyone sees the smoke, we can let on we're boiling them for ourselves."

"That should be the last thing we'd do," said Michael. "If old Morty sees the smoke and comes here, we're done." He looked around at the others sharply. "Not a word to anyone, now. I hope none of you talk in your sleep."

"No, no. Not a word. We won't tell anyone."

All the talk of food had made them hungry. From the

53

position of the sun, they knew it was dinner-time in everyone's house, and they could almost imagine that the smell of bacon and cabbage and potatoes was mixed with the smell of turf-smoke that was always drifting over the island.

Before leaving them, they looked through the chinks in the shelter walls at the foxes. They were still fast asleep, so close to each other that one could hardly see where they joined. Their noses were laid flat to the ground and their fur moved a little as they breathed evenly.

"We have a few hours to get them some food," Patsy said. "We can come here with it, right after dinner if we have it. We can all collect some."

They went back by the way that they had come, because they had not forgotten the donkey who would still be standing with his cart where they had left him.

The donkey was tired of waiting. They could tell it by the way his ears twitched, and by the shivers that ran up his legs. He was swinging his tail quickly from side to side like the pendulum of a clock, as he always did when he was angry. As soon as he saw them, he let out a long, wailing bray, showing all of his big yellow teeth and stretching his neck until he looked as if he were about to fly off the ground.

"Yes, yes, we're coming," said Séamus. "Wasn't it nice of us not to have loaded the stones on you before we left?"

They loaded them now, and took away the stones with which they had wedged the wheels of the cart. As soon as he felt himself freed, the donkey gave a prancing leap that nearly sent the white stones spinning off the cart again. Then he tried to run along the shore but it was too rough for this. He had to content himself with walking, taking each step as if he intended to make a hole in the island with his hoof.

The boys walked beside the cart. Colm carried one glass ball and Patsy had the other, for of course they could not trust them on the cart. Out on the road, the donkey broke into a trot. The stones bounced with a deafening sound and the axle clattered and rattled. At the school they stopped and heaved the stones over the wall. Then they all climbed on the cart and made the rest of the journey home in that way.

"We'll go back to the shelter separately," Patsy said. "Each of us can bring what food we can get. It would be better not to be seen going in a crowd. We'll learn how to do all these things as we go on."

5

After dinner Patsy looked out through his own doorway and saw Séamus staggering around the corner of his
house with a bucket of steaming potatoes in each hand.
Potatoes would fill up the foxes better than anything else,
he thought, and he remembered his own promise to the
donkey. He took a hot potato from the basket that was
still standing on the kichen table and brought it out to the
little field behind the house where the donkey was
grazing. He was still twitching his ears with temper but
he took the potato without snapping.

Patsy had two slices of cold meat in his pocket, wrapped
in a cabbage leaf. It had been easy to slip them in there,
but his mother's praise of him for eating so quickly had
made him feel like a thief. When he met the others at the
shelter an hour later, he found that they felt the same.

"My mother said that the wind must have given me an
appetite," Colm said.

"We're promised double rations tomorrow," said Séamus. "We can eat one lot ourselves, maybe. My father
said today that if this goes on he'll teach us the thatching
next year. That made me feel mean."

They emptied their pockets of the pieces of meat. Altogether it made up as much as would fill a dinner-plate. Séamus and Michael had an old bucket filled with potatoes as well. These were still warm, and when they were peeled and mixed with the meat, they looked quite appetizing.

Carefully they opened the shelter door. The big fox lifted his head. Now they could see that his eyes had brightened. His fur was no longer limp, but stood out around his neck like a huge collar.

"Are you sure they're not lions?" Colm whispered in Patsy's ear. "That looks like a mane to me."

"No, no. They're foxes all right. Please don't be afraid any more. They'll feel it if you are afraid and they'll be nervous of us all."

Patsy walked up to the big fox and stroked his head. Those eyes were as sharp as the prongs of a fork. There was a hard, bright light in them that was wild and marvellous. When he moved his head, Patsy could feel the strength of his neck. He was not frightened at all.

"They're tame, these foxes," he said. "They behave like dogs. We'll feed them in here."

They brought in the bucket of feed and spilled some out on a cleared place on the rock floor of the shelter. The big fox stood up and stretched himself. Then he walked over stiff-legged, and nosed at the warm potatoes. He took one cautiously, chewed it slowly as if he were noticing a new taste, and swallowed it down. He took another piece and ate that more quickly. Then he left the food and went across to the other fox. He poked her once with his nose. She stood up slowly and followed him back to the food, and they began to eat together, faster and faster, until they had finished everything. Then they licked the floor clean with their narrow, thin tongues until not a speck of food remained. When they were quite sure that there was no more, they went back to the heap of ferns and lay down again, and closed their eyes.

"When they wake up they'll want to go outside," Colm said. "Foxes are very clean, my Uncle Martin says. He says that proves that they're not animals at all but witches in disguise."

"We'd better get a length of rope for each of them," Patsy said. "If we put it on their necks now while they're still tired, we'll be able to lead them outside when they wake up."

"Couldn't we build a stockade all around the shelter? That's what people do on desert islands——"

"Those are the islands where there are plenty of trees. Here we have only furze. And the foxes would burrow under the stockade in no time. And the noise we would make in building it would bring the whole island down on us. And if they didn't come then they'd see our stockade from several fields away if they happened to be passing by——"

"All right, all right," said Michael. "No need to be so fierce. It was just an idea I had. Where will we get rope?"

Patsy had a piece which he had been keeping for the day when he would need it. Séamus knew where there was a piece, in the cowshed at home, that would not be needed until the next time that calves would be shipped to Galway.

"When those foxes wake up they'll be thirsty," Patsy said. "Now we must get to work on the stream."

"Bill-hooks," said Séamus.

They were silent for minute or two, thinking of them.

No one would lend a bill-hook to a boy. They were hung high in the cart-sheds so that no boy could reach them. As Patsy said, it seemed that everyone on the island believed that the first thing a boy would do with a bill-hook would be to cut off his own leg with it. That was what the men always said if they saw a boy put his hand near a bill-hook or a scythe:

"Don't touch that! Do you want to cut the leg off yourself?"

"There's no honest way of getting bill-hooks," said Patsy at last.

Michael said suddenly:

"Morty Quinn might have one, if we could find it. It would be in a cruel condition with rust, because Morty hasn't cut as much as a thistle for years."

"Could we use it rusty?"

"Of course. It would be easier to cut the brambles with a clean sharp bill-hook, but we may as well give up hoping for that."

"Mr. Thornton," said Patsy. "If he had a bill-hook, it would be clean and sharp."

But the others would not agree to ask for it and they would not take anything of Mr. Thornton's without his leave.

"He's a reasonable, decent man," said Séamus, "but I'm thinking even he wouldn't lend a bill-hook to a boy. Morty is our only chance. Who'll go for it?"

"I'll go," said Patsy. "The rest of you can be cutting the brambles with your knives until I come back."

Michael and Séamus had a knife each. Colm had none, because he was thought to be too small.

"And it's not as if I could cut off my leg with it," he

said bitterly. " 'Twould take a week to do that with a penknife."

Two knives between three meant that there was always one resting or taking away the brambles that had been cut. It was very slow with such weak implements and they had hardly cleared a foot of the boreen by the time that Patsy was back with the bill-hook.

"It was easy," he said. "It was high up, of course, like all bill-hooks, in the cart-shed. I climbed up on the old cart and got it down." He held it up for them to see. "The rust is only on the outside. It won't break."

"Did you see old Morty?"

"No. I heard him in the house, moving around, but he didn't come out."

The bill-hook was wonderful. They slashed with the blade and then pulled the brambles away with the hooked point, and in less than an hour they had cleared the way into the well. The middle of the boreen was soft grass, easy to walk on, because the roots of the brambles were all under the shelter of the walls.

By the time that they reached the well, they were hot and thirsty. The first thing that they did when they saw the shining water was to scoop it up in handfuls and drink it. Then Patsy fetched the potato bucket and they rinsed it in the stream and filled it with water. Very quietly they opened the shelter door and poured some of the water into a hollow in the stone floor. The big fox opened his eyes and looked at them but he did not move.

"We've thought of everything," Patsy said, when they came outside again. "Now we must go home for those ropes. We've thought of everything. If only there would be no fox-hunt, we could keep them safe for ever."

But that same evening, the men began to plan the fox-hunt in earnest. The wind had dropped still more.

"We can go fishing tomorrow evening by the looks of it," said Seán Mór. "I have my spuds all planted. How are they with you, Peter?"

"Tomorrow will finish them," said Peter. " 'Twasn't such a bad storm at all, though they say on the radio that there was a ship damaged hereabouts."

"A wreck?"

Everyone sat up eagerly.

"Not a wreck at all," said Peter. "It wasn't a big enough storm for that. They lost some deck cargo." He laughed. "If it comes our way, I'm thinking we won't be so thankful."

"Everything is good that comes from the sea," said Mike Hernon wonderingly.

"Not everything, Mike. We have enough and plenty of this kind of cargo already."

"Is it potatoes?"

"Is it rocks and stones? Sure, they'd sink to the bottom of the sea. What have we plenty of?"

"It's foxes!"

The boys moved closer together on their bench. Patsy gripped Michael's arm and squeezed it in and out until Michael pulled himself free.

"Foxes! Who would have a cargo of foxes?"

All the men laughed and Seán Mór said:

"If there's people willing to buy foxes, we'll all maybe be sending in herds of them to Galway on the tender, to sell at the fair."

There was a burst of laughter again at this notion. Peter said:

"These were special silver foxes, on their way to the zoo in Dublin. They belonged to a man who breeds them. He asked to have them sent back to him if anyone found them. But sure, they'd be dead and drowned by now. How could they live through that sea?"

"Foxes could live through a lot," said Seán Mór.

Nellie said:

"The poor man, to lose his foxes! I hope they'll be found and sent back to him."

"If they come here, they'll get a short welcome," said Mike. "A fox is a fox."

"Do you mean you'd kill the decent man's foxes!" Nellie was horrified at this.

"A queer kind of a man, that would keep foxes," said Mike. "How could he be a decent man?"

"A fox is a fox," said all the men. "Hunt them down— that's the only way with them."

" 'Tis a queer thing for a man to keep foxes, for sure," said Nellie, and Peter said:

"We'll take our time planning this hunt. When we're finished, there won't be a fox on the length or breadth of the island."

For the rest of the evening while they listened to the men planning the fox-hunt, the boys said not a single word.

The next morning was Sunday. Dressed in their stiff, clean Sunday clothes, after they came out of the church they walked a little distance down the road away from the crowds of people, and Patsy said:

"It's well that we hid our foxes. Did you hear the way they talked about them? They're hard-hearted, mean——"

"It isn't that at all," Séamus said. "My father talked about it last night. He said that when a man has his own house, and his wife and children to look after, he has to turn into a fighter. He has to beat off everything that would do harm to his family, everything that would steal their food and shelter. He has to know every trade so that he can do what's wanted in his own house and in the house of every poor widow as well, that has no one to look after her. That's why he's able to do building and carpentry

63

and thatching and fishing, as well as every kind of farming. That's why he has to hunt the foxes."

"Will we be like that?" Patsy said doubtfully.

"I'll never hunt," said Colm positively. "I'll have foxes and rabbits all sheltering in my kitchen and my wife cooking big pots of porridge for them."

"The foxes would prefer if she'd cook a rabbit for them," said Michael. "Everthing hunts something else."

"I don't want to think about that," Patsy said. "They can hunt the red foxes as they always did, but they should leave our foxes alone."

"We couldn't expect them to do that unless we tell them all about them."

No one wanted to tell about the foxes. It was not only that they liked to have them to themselves, to visit in secret and to feed and play with. They did not really believe that the men would ever trust foxes, no matter how tame, no matter what colour, no matter where they came from. Listening to them talk last night, the boys had learned this. Patsy said:

"If we stop minding those foxes, they won't last a week."

At once they began to wonder what had happened during the night.

"Perhaps they got frightened and broke down the door."

"Perhaps they got thirsty and broke out to get water."

"It's long past getting-up time for foxes. Perhaps they broke out because we didn't come at dawn."

"Perhaps old Morty walked over there early, and found them."

They looked at each other in despair, and began to run, heads down, one behind the other, up the road past all the houses, down the side-road just before Mr. Thornton's house and along the top of the wall by the stream. No one took any notice or asked them where they were running so fast and earnestly. They never asked the dogs either, when they ran in little, busy packs about their own business.

They reached the tiny field where the shelter was. They stood in a row and stared. The door was tightly shut, still tied with Patsy's string. There was no hole in the walls.

"We'll get their food ready first. Then we'll open the door. What have you got?"

Out of his own pocket Patsy took a slice of fresh white soda-bread with butter on it, and half of a rasher of bacon, rolled up. Colm had a raw egg, complete in its shell.

"I took it from the red hen this morning," he said. "I heard my mother scolding her afterwards, for not laying one. She's fond of the red hen, though, so she didn't threaten to make soup of her."

"An egg is good," said Michael. "Perhaps we can get seagulls' eggs and be beholden to no one for them."

He and Séamus had bread and jam, and a rasher each.

"Sunday morning we always have rashers," said Séamus. "I hope they won't be expecting this every morning."

"They'll eat one meal a day, like dogs," Patsy said. "These are only little extra bits to make them fond of us."

He went across to the shelter and untied the string that

held the hasp of the door shut. Then very slowly and carefully he opened the door a little so that they could all look in.

There in the dark they could see the foxes lying close together, looking towards the door with brilliant eyes. Colm

ran forward, four little steps, and then stopped. He knelt
and moved forward on his knees very slowly, stretching
out a gentle hand.

"Look!" he said in a whisper. "A cub. There are four of
them. Now we have a whole family of foxes!"

6

They moved softly into the shelter and knelt beside Colm. They lifted the cubs out one by one.

"Four of them, one for each of us," said Patsy. "And they're all strong and healthy. It's no wonder she was tired."

He stroked the mother fox's head until she closed her eyes and pressed against him.

"How did she live through the sea? She might have been drowned so easily."

They shivered with horror at this idea.

"She likes us," Patsy said. "She's not a bit snappy."

The cubs were burrowing under her, poking and nuzzling until they found where the milk was. Then they began to suck, first with little whines and squeaks and then quite silently.

"She'll look after their food for a few weeks," said Michael. "That's something. But when they are too old to live on milk, we'll have *six* foxes to feed."

It was a terrible thought, and yet it brought with it a feeling of strength as if they had all grown suddenly more powerful.

"Now I know how my father feels," Séamus said. "We'll just have to provide for those foxes."

"A whole family," Colm said. "I wish I could show them to my mother. She's a great hand with pups always, and these would be the same."

Patsy had been thinking of this too, but they had to agree again that no one was to be told.

"Sometime, we may be able to tell, but not now," Patsy said. "It's more important than ever for us to bring the stream this way. Six foxes will need plenty of water."

They went to look at the spring, bubbling in its little sandy well. The water flowed away in a deep narrow stream over stones, bordered with thickly growing grass. It made a heavy gurgling sound, the sound that Patsy had heard from the top of the wall yesterday.

"There is plenty of water there, sure enough," said Michael. "Will it be missed if we turn it all this way?"

"Not at all! The only house is Mr. Thornton's and he gets his water from the well behind his house. He doesn't even know that this well is here."

"He'll wonder why his stream dries up."

"He'll think it's the summer coming. He won't notice, when he never uses the water."

"When I was getting the bill-hook," Patsy said, "I saw two spades in Morty's shed. We'll need them now for digging the new channel for the stream."

"Surely he'll miss two spades!"

"There were cobwebs on them. I'd swear he never touches them. Sure, you know he doesn't even plant potatoes any more, only lives on what the neighbours leave in to him."

It was true that Morty, like other men who were too old to work, and the widows who had no one to work for them, was given a small share in everyone's food. A man would bring him some potatoes and cabbage, a woman would bake him a loaf of bread, another would keep him a piece of bacon, or a few eggs, so that he was never hungry.

"It's like giving to God himself," the people said, and they never grudged their charity.

Michael and Séamus went to get the spades. While they were gone, Patsy and Colm collected flat, smooth stones, with which to pave the new channel.

"We have no shortage of stones, anyway," said Colm. "They'll keep the water clean."

They planned to dig a round pond as well, and to line it with stones.

"It doesn't have to be deep," Patsy said. "The water can flow in by one side of it and out by the other. We could never do this if the land didn't slope towards the shelter. It will be slow enough making the channel."

"Not with four of us, and two spades," said Colm. "Two can dig and two can lay the stones. That way we'll be finished in no time at all."

But it was slow work. Michael and Séamus did the digging because they were the strongest and the oldest. The ground was hard. It had never been dug before and though the grass looked so soft and innocent, its roots were knotted toughly underground and had to be chopped and cut with the spades. These were blunt from lack of use. They had got lazy, Michael said, from an idle life.

Still, by dinner-time they had done a quarter of it, and had lined it ready for the water to flow. They had left a little piece of ground undug between the channel and the well. This was Patsy's idea.

"If we let the water through from the beginning, we'll

be working in mud. It will be better to dig it dry and let the water in last of all."

"Anyone would think you were turning streams every day of the week," said Séamus.

"I've done a lot of thinking," Patsy said. "Thinking is every bit as important as doing."

"That's what Mr. Thornton always says," said Colm. "I wish we could show all this to *him*."

"Not to anyone, not to anyone at all!" the others said.

They hardly spoke on the way home, practising for keeping quiet about the wonderful things that they were doing. At dinner-time Patsy's mother said:

" 'Tis a fine sunny day for you to be out enjoying yourself. Off with you again after dinner! Tomorrow there will be school."

And she gave him plenty of soda-bread and butter to keep him going until the evening. Leaving the house by the back way, he was able to take a bucketful of warm potatoes from the pigs' tub. When he reached the shelter he found the others had done the same.

"If we don't bring them plenty, they'll always have to get our rations," Michael said, showing his own parcel of bread and butter.

"I've been thinking," said Colm. "Maybe we shouldn't be digging the channel on Sunday. My father always says you get no blessing on what you dig on a Sunday——"

"That's only if you could just as well dig on a Monday. We can't—we'll be at school. I heard it in the church," Patsy said, "that if your cow or your donkey falls over a cliff, you can get them back on a Sunday. That covers our foxes too, you may be sure."

"I suppose so."

They worked steadily all the afternoon. No one came to this quiet corner of the island. Instead, all the Sunday walking was down towards the quay because the men were anxious about their boats. The wind was still strong but it was steady. Everyone said that if it held like this, Monday would be a day for fishing.

By six o'clock the narrow channel was finished and the round pool which was to be a drinking hole for the foxes. A second channel had to be made for the water to leave the pool, but there was no need to line this with stones. At last the moment came for cutting the little piece that still stood between the old stream and the new one.

Patsy was given the privilege of cutting this as the whole idea was his. The others gathered on the wall above, and Patsy chopped away the remaining sods. Quickly he placed the stones which were lying ready. At once the water began to pour itself into the new channel. The old stream was suddenly dry, though they saw its tail disappearing under the overhanging branches like a snake sliding away to cover.

They all ran along beside the advancing stream, watching it curl around the clean, white stones, darkening them and moving up the earth between them.

"It will be muddy for a while, of course," Patsy said. "Then all the loose earth will be washed away and it will be clear and good."

The water flowed into the pool. It seemed like an hour before it lay an inch deep on the stones. When they were sure that it was filling, Patsy said in a voice that was hoarse with excitement and fear:

"I thought it was all going to flow away into the

ground. I thought it would never, never lie in the pool."

Suddenly he leaped into the air and gave a great bellow of joy, like a donkey braying on a fine morning. Séamus pulled at his jersey and said:

"Quiet! Do you want the whole population coming to see what you're so pleased about?"

"I forgot," said Patsy. "Look at it! When the pool fills up, the water will flow out by the other channel. I wish I could spend all my life doing this."

" 'Twould be a great life, for sure."

As they sat and watched it slowly filling, Séamus said:

"Now we have everything ready. But I'll never sleep easy until those foxes are gone off this island. What was the name of that place where they were going?"

"The zoo in Dublin."

"What's that?"

"A place where all kinds of animals live, lions and tigers and wolves and elephants and giraffes and monkeys and camels—"

"Most of them in cages," said Colm, "though not all. My uncle Martin went there once. A beautiful garden with flowers, and all the animals well-fed and comfortable, with their own servants to look after them."

" 'Tis hard to believe," said Séamus, "but I suppose there are queerer things in the world than that. And they'd treat our foxes right if they had them there?"

"They'd have the life of Reilly," said Patsy. "My father went there once, and they were giving fish to the seals. It gave him a pain in his stomach to look at them guzzling the fish, he said, and we shooting seals every chance we get for eating fish around the islands. They'd

73

know the right food for these foxes and they'd give them the right kind of place to live in."

"It couldn't be better than here!"

"For the winter they'd have a warm house," Patsy said. "That's one thing we couldn't give them."

" 'Tis true. And no one would hunt them."

"We must write a letter."

"What was the man's name?"

No one could remember. Colm said:

"We'll just write: 'To the Man that Lost Foxes, The Zoo, Dublin.' He'll get our letter, all right."

"They must be different sort of people altogether in that zoo," said Séamus. "Most people, when they see an animal running, they want to shoot it dead at once, the way that a dog wants to chase a cat and a cat wants to chase birds. To bring plates of food to lions and tigers and foxes—that goes against nature for certain sure."

"Aren't we bringing plates of food to our foxes?" Patsy pointed out. "And they breed lions in that zoo in Dublin, my uncle said, and sell the cubs around the world—"

"Could anyone buy one?" Colm asked.

"Other zoos buy them, I suppose. They have a name for being healthy, the Dublin lions. They're walking around as free as ourselves."

"I wouldn't go near that zoo for Ireland free," said Michael positively. "Imagine turning a corner and finding a lion staring you in the face, and you having to persuade him that his dinner was at home in his house and there was no need for him to go foraging abroad."

"The lions are walking free but there are streams and walls around their place," Patsy said. "If there weren't, they'd take an odd stroll into Dublin now and then, for a change of diet. You'd think your sense would tell you that."

"I was thinking Dublin must be a dangerous place altogether," said Michael.

"Now, what will we write in the letter?"

"I know," said Patsy. "It's in our book at school. We're just at it now. I wish we had a piece of paper handy."

No one had a piece of paper but they made up what would be in the letter all the same.

"Up in the right-hand corner we'll put 'Inishownan, Galway Bay.' Then over on the left: 'Dear Sir.' That's the way all letters begin."

"What about if it was a woman?" Colm demanded. "How would she like to be called 'Dear Sir'?"

"There's a way of writing to her, too. You'll come to it in the book in a year or two," Patsy said. " 'Dear Sir, we have your foxes here safe and sound, only now it's six foxes instead of two because there are cubs.' "

"Tell him they're happy and contented," Colm said in a half-whisper, almost as if the owner of the foxes was listening.

"Yes, that's a good idea. 'They are happy and contented and are eating well. The four cubs are healthy.' "

"What will we do if he writes and asks us to send them on to him? If we get a letter, everyone will want to know what's in it."

"He must come for them himself," Patsy said. "We'll tell him that. 'The people on this island don't like foxes —' "

" 'Except us,' " Colm interrupted.

" 'Except us. We found them on the shore and we have

75

them hidden in a safe place. But we're afraid that if the people find them they will kill them, because they don't like foxes.' "

"You said that before."

"Well, it's true. If they knew we had them here, they'd be expecting every misfortune to fall on the island."

"The men are going fishing tomorrow," Séamus said.

"We know it's only superstition," Patsy said, after a pause.

But they all wished that Séamus had not reminded them of the fishing. Patsy said that their sense should tell them that the men would not be any safer on the sea if they killed the family of foxes first.

"Sense, sense!" Michael said angrily. "You're always talking about sense. Don't you know well that sense has nothing to do with this? If the men were to kill the foxes, they wouldn't feel any safer. Feeding them and keeping them—they'd think that was like keeping a pet devil. How do we know how much truth is in what they believe? There must be some sense behind it, whatever you say."

"My mother says that maybe a fox once caused a boat to sink, some long time ago," Patsy said. "If a man took a fox in a boat, taking him to another island to kill the rabbits, maybe, and if the fox jumped out and frightened the people and was the cause of the boat overturning, she said, people would remember that and hold it against all foxes for ever after."

"That's sense, that could happen, indeed," the others said.

" 'This means that you can't write us a letter,' " Patsy went on. " 'Just come with a boat as soon as you can and we'll have your foxes safe and sound for you.' "

"How can we promise him that?" Séamus said. "If

76

someone finds them before he comes, they won't be safe and sound."

"We'll put in another bit, then. 'If you don't come quickly, something may happen to them. It is very hard to mind a family of foxes.'"

"That will be fine," they all said. "That will bring him quickly, if he wants them back."

"Of course he wants them back. I wonder what kind of a man is he."

Patsy thought he would look rather like a fox, but it did not matter very much what he looked like so long as he came and went quickly.

"That's another thing," Patsy said. "I'll say: 'When you come, please don't tell anyone what you have come for. Just ask for me. I'll call my friends and we will lead you to the place where the foxes are.'"

"Could he take them away without being seen?"

"We won't think of that, until the time comes," said Patsy. "I'll write the letter this evening because I heard the men saying that it's likely the Post Boat will come to-morrow if the wind is down."

"Where will we get a stamp?"

No one had thought of this until Séamus said it. They looked at each other eagerly, knowing that they would be able to tell at once if anyone had fourpence. No one had. They never needed money, but in any case everyone's mother had ten things to spend fourpence on, besides giving it to boys.

"We'll have to take one from the Post Office without being seen."

"More stealing!" Colm said furiously. "I hate it. Isn't there any honest way to get a stamp?"

"No. But it will be more like borrowing than stealing," said Patsy, "because when the man comes for his foxes, he can pay it back. He is quite certain to have fourpence."

Before they left them to go home, they brought the foxes out to drink from the pool. As soon as she had finished, the mother fox went straight back to the shelter again.

"If she hadn't those cubs, she would be wanting to wander," Séamus said. "Knowing that she must feed them will keep her contented here for a few weeks."

"I'll write the letter this evening," Patsy said, "and I'll get the stamp in the morning when I go for stamps for my mother. She'll surely write to my aunts in America this evening, when she knows that the Post Boat will be here tomorrow."

7

That evening, all over the island everyone was writing letters. Patsy took a sheet of paper from one of his own exercise books and wrote his letter exactly as they had planned. When he had finished it he read it through. It certainly showed there was need to hurry, that the foxes were in danger every day that they stayed on the island.

It seemed to Patsy that as soon as it would reach him, the owner of the foxes would not delay a moment before getting a boat and coming to fetch them away. He tried to count up the days that would have to pass before he would come sailing into the quay at Inishownan, but this was impossible. There would be days for the letter to travel, and days for the men to find a boat, and days for him to get people to come with him. There was nothing to do but wait.

In the morning, before school, his mother gave him half a crown and said:

"Down to the Post Office with you and get me two stamps, one for Aunt Maggie in Boston, and one for Aunt Maria in Portland."

She gave him two letters and told him to stick the two stamps well, because if they fell off, the Boston people or the Portland people might say that they had never been put on at all and they might think that the Irish were a dishonest nation. She told him to be sure to ask Seán the Post for the little blue stamp that you get for nothing and that tells that the letter is to go by aeroplane. These were to be stuck in the left-hand corner and he was to stick them very well too, because the gum wasn't strong, being free. And she promised to pray for the pilot of the aeroplane every night for a year, in the rosary, in return for his trouble.

Patsy had the two letters in his hand when he reached the Post Office, but he had his own in his pocket for safety's sake. It was well for him that he had.

Seán the Post was not there. Patsy could hear him in the telegraph room working his little machine. This surely meant that the Post Boat was coming, though the wind was still fierce enough. Seán's wife Kate was at the table in the kitchen where the stamps were kept. She loved selling stamps, though she was not allowed to keep the money. That had to be sent into Galway, every penny of it, but Kate had the satisfaction of counting it and handling it at least. She always looked happy on the day when the Post Boat came.

"Come on in, agrá," she called out when she saw Patsy standing by the door. Her eyes shone like a seagull's eyes, round and yellow. "Come on in, with your letters."

He came in and asked for two stamps for America, and he put the half-crown on the table. She picked it up with her left hand and took the two letters neatly from him with her right.

"Maria in Portland and Maggie in Boston," she said. "Fine girls they were, the two of them, always glad to hear news from home and they exiles in a foreign land. I wonder now, did she tell them how the sow died on her in the cold weather?"

She cocked an eye at Patsy but he was too well-trained for her.

"Maybe," he said. "I didn't read the letter."

"Maybe she did, then," said Kate. "Sometimes if you'd tell a thing like that to the people in America, the next thing is that a little packet of dollars would be coming for you."

Patsy felt himself getting hot.

"We have a slip of a sow growing up instead of the one that died," he said.

"You have, agrá, you have, indeed," said Kate. She held the letters up to the light as if she would like to read them through the envelopes. Then she dropped them on the table and said with a sigh: "I suppose I'd better give you your stamps."

She took the stamp book from the table drawer and laid it on the table. Patsy looked over her shoulder, through the small window that gave on to the back field. Suddenly he shouted in a tone of horror:

"A cat! A huge black cat, after your chickens!"

Kate was as round and as wide as a wash-tub but she was quick on her feet. She flashed around the end of the table, seized the sweeping-brush that stood by the door and darted outside and around the corner of the house. Patsy leaned across and tore off a fourpenny stamp and slipped it in his pocket. Then he went to the door to meet Kate on her way back.

She came in panting, trailing the sweeping-brush.

"He was gone, the blackguard," she said. "Thanks to you. There's no end to his hunger. He's watching my birds and I'm watching him for the last fortnight. I'm thinking he'll get one of them yet on me."

Any other woman on the island would have cut him a slice of bread at once, as a reward for his warning. Kate just said:

"I'd best give you your stamps. You're on your way to school, I suppose."

She made him leave the two letters on the table, although he could see the post-bag lying on the floor behind her with its mouth open.

On the way to school he met Michael and Séamus and told them what had happened.

"And the letter is still here in my pocket," he said, "though it's something to have a stamp on it."

"If we miss the boat this time, we might have those

foxes to look after for months to come," said Michael.

"We won't miss the boat."

The school was always closed while the Post Boat was at the quay. The boys heard its hooter first as they were putting away their books at lunch-time.

"The post!" Mr. Thornton said. "A race! Who'll get there first?"

He opened the door of the school and the boys all emptied out into the playground. Colm was the first out through the gateway, as he always was, leaping down the hill to the sea so fast that the movement of his legs could scarcely be seen. When the others reached the quay, he was already standing there, looking out at the boat.

It was a motor launch, the size of the Aran life-boat. Just now its engine was switched off and it was a few yards out from the quay wall, bouncing up and down on the wicked little waves. Only a patch of water six feet wide was protected by the quay. Two currachs were tied at the steps, sheltering close under the wall like dogs crouching in shelter from a shower of rain.

Willie, the captain of the Post Boat, was standing forward when the boys arrived. His mate, indeed his whole crew, Mike, was whirling a wet rope to throw ashore. Seán the Post was there, waiting to catch it. While they watched, Willie threw the rope. The wind caught it and sent it straight up into the air. Mike hauled it in and threw it again. The same thing happened. Mike threw it again but it was quite clear that that rope was not going to come ashore until the wind dropped.

Seán the Post never went to sea. He spent all his time with his stamps and his telegraph, and all he knew about boats was as much as he remembered from his young days.

Now he began to run up and down the quay, calling out to Willie:

"Let you wait! Let you wait there awhile and some of the men will be down for certain sure. I have no one here, only a pack of boys."

"I will not wait," Willie bawled back at him. He seemed to have lost his temper with Seán, as if he should have tied up the wind in good time for the Post Boat to land. "We'll try one throw more, and if that doesn't reach you, we'll be off until the wind drops in a few weeks' time."

"My bags of mail!" Seán shouted. "What about them?"

"We'll come for them in a few weeks. You can keep them safe. Sure, nothing ever happens on Inishownan anyway, as all the world knows. I don't know what ye want with letter-writing."

"I'll report you for this!"

"My instructions are that I'm to land if the weather permits it," Willie shouted back. "You needn't

bother to report it, for I'll be doing that myself."

Suddenly Patsy saw that Séamus had gone down the steps and boarded one of the currachs. He cast off, took the oars and sent the currach out towards the Post Boat. It all happened so fast that he had almost reached it before Seán noticed him. When he did, he stood on the quay wall as near as he could to the edge and yelled:

"Good boy, Séamuisín! There's a man for you! Drop him the rope, Mike. Drop it down to him. Now back with you—come on—come on——"

Séamus could not hear a word of this, of course, with the sound of the wind and the waves. He had the rope on board in a flash, however, as if he were following Seán's instructions. Quickly he slipped it around his wrist and began to row back to the steps.

While every eye was fastened on Séamus and on what he was doing, Patsy quietly opened the mail-bag nearest to him and dropped his letter inside. Then he turned back to watch how Séamus was getting on.

As soon as the rope was in the currach, Willie had started up his engine again. Slowly he moved in towards the quay. Séamus rowed faster but he was rowing against the wind. Just by the steps the Post Boat caught up with him. Séamus flicked the rope ashore. Seán caught it and gave a shout:

"Out! Out, or you'll be crushed!"

For one terrible moment it looked as if the launch was going to flatten the currach against the quay wall. But Séamus had seen what was happening. Quickly he pushed the currach to safety by pressing his hands against the quay wall. Just before the Post Boat came alongside, he was free. Mike's white face looked down at him and Mike's long drawl sang out:

"I thought you were finished, so I did. I thought we'd make mincemeat out of you."

Willie looked frightened too but he only showed it by shouting at Séamus:

"Don't you know anything about boats? Anyone would think 'twas your first time in a currach."

Séamus said nothing. He had had a fright, as Patsy could see, and it was likely that the only answer he could have given would have been an uncivil one. However, in a moment he was forgotten. Mike came ashore and took the mail-bags. Michael and Patsy and Colm watched him heave them into the boat, with the bags which had already been collected from the other islands.

"Now it's safe," Michael whispered.

Seán was inviting Willie up to the Post Office for dinner.

"I may as well come," Willie said. "Though I was thinking there a while ago that I'd be making my dinner with Mike out of a few herring he caught on the way out."

He climbed ashore and stood for a second on the quay to shout back at Mike:

"Let you mind the boat till I come back in an hour, or maybe in two hours." He turned to Seán. "The day I don't have spuds for my dinner I don't feel I've had a right dinner at all."

" 'Tis true for you, indeed," said Seán. "I feel the same myself."

He picked up the incoming bag of mail, slung it over his shoulder and started up the quay with Willie. Mike spat into the sea and said sourly:

"A herring and a bit of bread is good enough for Mike, of course, but my Lord must have his spuds. No one said a word about coming back in a while and letting me off to have a few spuds too."

"We'll bring you down some," Michael said. "I'll run all the way with them and that way they won't get cold."

"Good boy, good boy," said Mike. "I'll be frying the herrings while you're getting them. I suppose I could boil a few spuds too, if I wanted to, but they'd be too slow."

"That man won't starve while he has a tongue in his head," Michael said, as they started for home. "All his talk of herrings and bits of bread—I wouldn't be able to eat a bite of my dinner if I hadn't promised him some of it."

The day of the post was almost like a holiday on the island. In every kitchen, visitors were continually dropping in to give their own news of their people in America and to hear the news of the family that they were visiting. Kettles boiled all afternoon, fresh pots of tea were made and long slices of soda-bread buttered for the visitors. By evening the boys had collected enough soda-bread to feed the foxes for a whole day. They felt well pleased with themselves when they settled on their bench in Patsy's house after dark, to listen to the evening talk.

" 'Twas a grand day, thank God," said Seán Mór when he had welcomed all his visitors and had seen them seated comfortably. "The Post Boat to come safely and to-morrow looking good for the fishing. Mike and Willie said you could nearly take the herring in with your cap."

" 'Tis a gentleman's life," said Peter, "fishing tomorrow, fox-hunting the day after. We'll have to send the word around that the dogs are to be ready."

"What kind of dogs will you hunt with?" asked Mr. Thornton, who was sitting on the hob, looking quite comfortably at ease.

"Every class and kind of dog," said Seán. "We're not a bit particular—terriers and collies and mixtures of the two."

"Will collies hunt foxes for you?"

"They love it, man. 'Tisn't good for their character, I suppose. They get a fancy for hunting and sometimes then they want to hunt the sheep."

"Are they good on the scent?"

"Not bad at all. They're the best we have, anyway. We have to have dual-purpose dogs, like the Department of Agriculture's cows."

Everyone laughed at this idea. Mr. Thornton said:

"A piece of rotten meat or rotten fish breaks the scent."

"It does so. Rotten fish is the worst—the dogs won't cross the scent of rotten fish."

"There's a dead shark thrown up on the shore below my house this last fortnight," said Mr. Thornton, "but I suppose the foxes don't go down by the sea much."

"In the rocks, especially up at the Fort, that's where they like to be," said Seán Mór. "We'll give them a good run, you may be sure, the blackguards."

And they began to talk of the damage that had been done by foxes in the last week. The boys dared not look at each other. The heat of the fire and the loud talk made

89

Patsy's head buzz. He was glad that the men went away early, to prepare their fishing gear.

In the morning, the boys were all early at the shelter, though they had had no chance to arrange this. Before anyone had time to speak, Séamus said:

"The bill-hook will do. And we have an old sack."

The others knew at once what he was talking about. Colm said:

"Need we all go?"

"No," said Patsy quickly. "You stay here and help to feed the foxes. Two will be enough to go."

Michael and Séamus agreed that they should go together, because anyone meeting them with their sack would think that they were on a family message.

Though Patsy would not have refused to go for the piece of rotten shark-meat, he was glad to be left behind with Colm. They brought soda-bread to the foxes and then led them out to drink from the pool which was now quite full. They could see that the cubs had grown even since yesterday. Their eyes were bright like little wet shells and their soft ears seemed far too big for them. Already they had a look of not trusting anyone.

It was half an hour before Michael and Séamus were back, swinging the sack between them.

"If this doesn't keep the dogs away, nothing will," Michael said. "It gave us all we could do to cut off a piece, and to have to carry it after that was a torment."

"Maybe the foxes won't like it either," Colm said. "They're related to dogs, I've heard people say. Perhaps they'll go wild when they smell it."

"We'll keep it well out from the shelter."

They carried the sack to the edge of the little field

90

where the shelter stood and then they dragged it along the ground, circling the shelter several times around.

" 'Twill be a tough dog that will cross that," Séamus said. "We'll hardly be able to cross it ourselves."

They washed their hands in the stream where it left the pool and dried them on the grass. Then they hid the sack of shark-meat in the brambles by the wall and ran back to be in time for school.

8

The day of the fox-hunt was a terrible one for the boys. It was clear and sunny but the wind was strong enough to blow white caps on the waves far out to sea. It was a west wind, and it went shouting and roaring around the school, sending the soft turf ash up the chimney with the sparks and the smoke. It carried sounds suddenly, in spurts, sometimes too loud and sometimes so faintly that one could not judge their distance.

All morning long, the boys heard the light excited barking of the dogs, and the voices of the men calling to them. They could not concentrate on their sums and their geography and history. All they could think of was dogs and foxes. Mr. Thornton got quite angry, which happened very seldom. He made them shut all the windows, but still the sounds came through, more irritating than ever because of being harder to hear.

At eleven o'clock, Séamus said desperately:

"Mr. Thornton, may I go for a can of water, please? I'm thirsty."

"There is water in the can, Séamus," Mr. Thornton said. "I filled it myself this morning."

"It's empty now, sir," said all the boys together.

Mr. Thornton looked directly at Patsy, but he did not ask if he had emptied away the water. Patsy saw Colm looking over from the other side of the school, where the small boys sat, and he guessed that it was he who had done it. Then Mr. Thornton said an extraordinary thing. The boys could hardly believe their ears. Good, kind Mr. Thornton, who was always so gentle even with the few boys who were troublesome, said:

"Someone emptied away the water that I brought this morning, so there will be no playtime at twelve o'clock. Instead, everyone will sit and eat his lunch, and we'll go on about Brian Boru and the battle of Clontarf."

And there they had to sit, until at last they heard the crowd of men and dogs pass excitedly right by the school on their way home. Only then did Mr. Thornton say:

"That's enough for today."

Everyone went out without a word, and Mr. Thornton looked so busy with his books that no one dared to speak to him.

"I planned it all with Colm," Séamus said on the way home. "I'd have put the can down by the well and I'd have run like the wind to see if the foxes were safe."

"What good would that have done?" Patsy said. "Even now it would be no use going to see them, until our usual time. If anything has happened to them, we'll hear it the moment we get home. We'll go at our usual time."

When they reached Patsy's house, a crowd was still gathered there, slow to go home after the excitement of the morning.

"Five foxes we got," Peter said, delighted with a new audience when the boys came in. "We never got five in a morning before, nor I don't think our fathers nor our grandfathers did either."

" 'Twas a great day, for sure," said Seán Mór. "We can sleep easy at night now, without fearing that those red scoundrels will be rifling the hen-houses unknown to us."

"Ay, they'll keep out from us, the ones that's left," Peter boasted. "You may be sure they're above there in their burrows going over and over the story of what happened to their comrades."

"Enough of that, now, enough!" said Seán Mór, seeing that Patsy was pitying those frightened foxes. "Back to work, or we won't have a bite to give the same hens, and 'twill be as bad for them to die of starvation as feeding the foxes."

When the men had gone, he said gently to Patsy:

"We can't let them increase and multiply and fill the whole island."

"I know," Patsy said, but he was thinking of Father Fox going off with his little bag for flour and never coming home any more.

It was certain now that their foxes were safe. If they had been found, it would have been the first thing they would have heard. Still, Patsy shivered with terror for them as he came near the shelter later in the afternoon. The smell of the rotten shark-meat reached him on the wind. He hoped that it had kept the dogs a good way off, because even safe in the shelter the foxes would have known they were sniffing and nosing about. Perhaps they had heard the dogs, indeed, for they were huddled together in the far corner of the shelter when the door was opened. They soon came sliding forward to eat, however, and then they seemed to forget their fears.

94

The cubs were like new-born pups, with short, thin legs that looked as if they would never be able to carry the weight of their bodies.

"They're quiet now," Séamus said, "but in a few weeks they'll be rolling and nipping and growling and yapping. That's when we'll have the trouble."

"Perhaps the man will come very soon," said Colm, "before they're able to make much noise."

But days and days passed, and still he did not come. It seemed that the cubs grew twice as much by night as by day. Every morning the boys were shocked to see how big they were and how lively. At first they just lay there, or dragged themselves nearer to their mother to get at her milk. But within ten days they were all standing up, trotting around like tiny horses, thumping with their forefeet, darting at each other, pulling each other's tails. It was beautiful to watch. The boys would have stayed with them all day if they had not had so many other things to do. Even while they were at school and doing all their usual tasks at home, they could never forget them for as much as a single minute.

One afternoon when they brought the two big foxes out to eat, one of the cubs came forward too and took a piece out of the dish. Séamus said:

"I know what that means. Their mother hasn't enough milk for them now. They've got too big."

"We'll never be able to get milk for them," Patsy said positively. "That's one thing I can't go near, the crocks of milk."

It was the same with all of them. In every house, the milk was treated with such care and respect that only the mother of the family ever attended to it. All the children

95

were able to milk the cows, of course, but they had to account for every drop. If they were to take some out on the way home, the cow would immediately be suspected of cutting down her supply, or else the milker would be told he had not done his job properly. Getting the last of the milk from the cow was very important, so that she would be encouraged to give plenty the next time. Usually an older person finished the milking, therefore, and this left no opportunity for removing some before it reached the house.

Once it got into the kitchen there was no hope at all. An exact amount was put into big jugs on the dresser, for the family's needs. Some was put in buckets for the calves, and the remainder went into the tall wooden dash-churn, to make butter. It would sometimes have been possible to take some from the churn, but this was usually sour and would not do for the cubs.

"We got so many things from old Morty Quinn, it's a pity his old cow died," said Michael. "In the latter end, he never milked her dry. We could have finished the job for him every day and he'd have been none the wiser."

"She's dead, so it's no use talking about her," said Patsy, "and I don't know any other cow like her."

No one else knew of a neglected cow either. Séamus said:

"I've been thinking this was going to happen for the past week or more. There's only one thing we can do."

"What's that?"

"Take a few cupfuls from every cow on the island. We'll have to be up early in the morning to get to the cows before the women come out to milk. We can be very quick. The first of the milk always comes quickly."

"If we're seen!"

"We'd better not be seen. If any of us is seen milking a neighbour's cow on the quiet in the early morning, our family will be disgraced for generations to come."

"I don't like it! I don't like it!" said Colm.

"What can we do?" Séamus asked. "We can't watch the cubs getting thinner every day, for want of food. It will never be missed. We won't be depriving anyone of much milk. The trouble will be to do it without being caught."

They agreed that only Michael and Séamus should go after milk for the cubs. Their father, Mike Hernon, owned land in three different parts of the island, and anyone seeing one of his boys walking along with a can would think that he had been sent to milk a cow in a distant field.

"And it won't be for long," said Patsy to Colm. "Surely the man must come soon. That letter told him that his foxes are in danger. If he cares for them at all, he'll surely come soon."

This put a new idea into their heads, that perhaps the man had not been pleased to know of the four cubs' arrival and that he no longer wanted his foxes back. But when they had played with the cubs a little longer they knew that this was impossible. Anyone who had ever seen fox cubs, as the owner of the foxes must have done, would know that there was nothing more marvellous in the world. Surely knowing that they were there would bring him all the more quickly.

Now, when they came near the shelter, they could always hear the cubs barking. It was a high, clear bark, like a laugh, and no one hearing it would mistake it for a dog's bark. Fortunately it was not very loud yet, be-

cause the cubs were so small. They were perpetually hungry, watching anxiously while the milk was poured for them and then flopping into it as if they had not drunk for a week. Their big ears were always cocked high and they had a trick of twitching them as if it helped them to hear better. They did this, and stared with their shining eyes, when the boys talked among themselves.

"It would almost make you believe the stories that they are really people," Patsy said one morning as they were going to school, "the way they look at us as if they understood every word."

Mr. Thornton had often told them how wrong it was to believe in superstitions about bad luck. God would not let a house fall down on you just because you met a red-haired woman or a black cat. It was wrong and silly, Mr. Thornton said, not to trust God's sense better than that. And still Patsy remembered so many, many stories about foxes that could talk, foxes that could make themselves invisible and slip into a kitchen at night and hear what you were saying about them, that he just could not have said a word against them even when they were not there, even if he had wanted to.

"They're never done talking of foxes in our house," Séamus said. "They say we'll never have a day's luck until we get the last fox off the island. That's what they want now, they did so well the day of the hunt."

"There will always be foxes on the island," Patsy said. "No matter how many they catch, there will always be a few that will hide."

That same day, the Post Boat arrived. It had no trouble in landing this time because the wind had dropped at last. The fat sacks were heaved up on to the quay and Willie said sorrowfully:

"I'm thinking I have no excuse to stay with ye for dinner today. Couldn't ye rise an old storm, somehow, and I'd have to come ashore until it's gone down again?"

"Faith and you're not so complimentary when you have to stay," said Seán the Post.

He needed help with the bags. Séamus and Michael were able to take one each but Patsy was too small. Still, he followed the others into the Post Office in the hope that he would not be noticed. But Kate said in a loud hearty voice:

"This is a busy day here. No time for chat."

And she took the bags and dumped them by the chair where she always sat, so that she would be able to go through them at her ease.

"A bite of bread for the boys, Kate!" said Seán the Post. "Didn't you see how they carried up the bags for me?"

"I did, sure," said she with a sigh, getting up and going

99

to the dresser. "There was a time when you could have carried them all yourself."

" 'Tis true for you," said Seán sadly.

Kate cut only two slices of bread, one each for Michael and Séamus. Patsy slipped outside and waited. When the others came out he said:

"May she never go in want. Thanks be to God I can get a bite to eat at home any time I need it."

They were all longing to know if the owner of the foxes had done as he was told, or if he had written them a letter. If one of the boys were to get a letter, ten heads would be peeking over his shoulder while he read it. They waited for a while, sitting on the garden wall. The heavy smell of the wallflowers was all around them and the bees hummed busily in and out. They knew that if Kate were to come on a letter for one of them, she would run out with it at once and demand to have it opened without delay.

She did not come. After a while they got down off the wall and started home for dinner. They looked out to sea but there was no sign of a strange boat. Suddenly they all felt the load of responsibility as if it would never be lifted from them. They could not look at each other. No one had the courage to say what they all felt, that perhaps their judgment in keeping the foxes had been wrong, that their own people would be rightly angry with them for keeping and protecting such a well-known enemy.

In the afternoon, it seemed that the cubs had grown even bolder. Certainly they were stronger. They skipped and jumped all round the shelter, exercising their muscles. The parents ran and played with them, circling them and knocking them over, holding them in ridiculous positions

with their paws while the cubs snapped and growled. To-day the boys could not simply enjoy them. They had begun to think too far ahead and to see one after another the difficulties that were before them.

Silently they went home. The same thought was grow-ing in all their minds. As long as it was there, they could not bring themselves to talk.

In the evening, they sat quite still on their bench in Patsy's house. No one noticed them. The house was crowded, and everyone was in high good humour over a letter that had come on the Post Boat. Every man that came into the kitchen was handed the letter to read, so that it was quite worn out before the evening was over. In any case, as Colm's father, Peter, pointed out, there was no need for them to read it because Seán Mór was telling them what was in it while they were reading. Also, the letter was written in English, and the men were never quite happy in that strange language, though they knew it was useful for writing letters in and for people who went to school.

The letter was from a lawyer in Galway. A certain Patrick O'Flaherty had died at a great age in Boston, having made a fortune in the building business.

"And just as will happen to us all," Seán Mór said, "he had to leave his pile of money behind him when he went to heaven, God be merciful to him."

"Amen," said everyone.

"And he hadn't chick nor child, so it all comes back to Inishownan where he came from, to everyone that can lay claim to be his cousin. And that's nearly every man on the island!"

"Glory be to God! Sure, 'tis true for you. There's hardly a one of us that hasn't a drop of O'Flaherty blood in him somewhere. Does it say we have to be close relations?"

"Not a word about that. 'Twill be a couple of hundred dollars for nearly every family. This is a year of luck for us and no mistake."

The whole evening went on working out who the ancient Patrick O'Flaherty was. At last it was agreed that he must have been very young when he left the island, or else a person who thought of no one but himself, since he had left no memory of his good deeds behind him. It was the like of these—selfish, hard-working, secretive, scrupulous men—that made fortunes in this world, the company said. A decent, generous man will never die rich. But they said it was well there were always plenty of big-hearted

102

people ready to spend the money when its owner had gone to glory.

They went home very late, and Patsy was glad of this because he was so tired that he fell asleep the moment he got into bed.

But in the morning, the problem of the foxes was still there. At the shelter, Patsy said:

"We're coming every day now for a month or more. No one has seen us yet, but that luck couldn't last for ever. Some day soon, someone will wonder what brings us here. Then it will be all up with our foxes."

"We can't keep them for ever," Séamus said. "Now there are six. Maybe next year there will be twelve, or even more."

"Count them up," said Michael. "Four cubs for each of the female cubs: that's eight cubs——"

"And these six," said Colm.

"That's fourteen. And four for the big foxes: that's eighteen. At this rate, the floor will be too small to hold them all."

"There's no use in trying to keep this up," said Patsy. "At least not by ourselves. We must have a grown-up person to help us."

"Mr. Thornton," said the others, all together.

"He's the only one," Patsy said. "We'll ask him today. He's the only one in the whole island that understands about foxes."

9

All morning long, they watched Mr. Thornton and imagined how he would receive the news about the foxes. They knew that he would listen quietly. There was no one like Mr. Thornton for that. People who listen can learn, he always said. Chatterers hear no one but themselves.

It was agreed that Patsy would do the talking, since Mr. Thornton already knew from reading his story that he did not hate foxes, as the islandmen did.

At lunch-time, Séamus said:

"We'll walk home with him when school is finished. There will be time to tell him everything on the way."

But Patsy said:

"We'll give him time to finish his dinner first. He's probably as hungry as we are, at the end of school. Hungry people only take in half of what they hear."

There was sense in this, the others said. They met after dinner at Patsy's house and began to walk to Mr. Thornton's. From time to time, one of them would say: "We'll tell him—" and stop. There were so many things to tell him and they were all things that he might not understand.

His house stood alone, far beyond the last of the village houses. Today it seemed as if they would never reach it, they were in such a hurry to get help, and yet when they came near it they went more and more slowly. They stopped altogether at the little bridge across the stream.

"The stream is dry," said Colm in astonishment.

"Of course it is," said Patsy. "Didn't we turn it the other way?"

Patsy was first over the bridge and up to Mr. Thornton's door. He was sitting by the fire, reading. Molly Conneeley, who came to cook and clean for him every day, was washing up at the table with a great clatter.

"Come in, boys," said Mr. Thornton. "Molly, some bread and jam."

She stopped her washing up at once to get four slices ready. They could not say what brought them as long as she was there. The bread and jam filled in the time very well. Mr. Thornton did not ask why they had come. He seemed to think it was just a friendly visit. He talked about his bees, and said that he thought of bringing the hives down to the school so that everyone would learn how to keep bees.

Molly put the last cup on the dresser and said:

"Good-bye, now, sir. I'll be back at six o'clock to make your tea."

There was a pause when she had gone. Then Patsy said:

"Mr. Thornton, we came to ask you to help us."

Mr. Thornton said, very quietly:

"Is it about the foxes?"

"You knew about them?"

"I went to see where my stream had gone to. Tell me all about them."

So Patsy began at the beginning and told how they had seen the two big foxes swimming and had brought them to the shelter, and how the cubs had arrived soon afterwards. He told how they had written and posted the letter to their owner.

"But he doesn't come, and the hunger devil is inside in those foxes," said Patsy. "Three loaves a day and a bucket of potatoes wouldn't satisfy them now. We have to steal milk from the cows for them. And every day we're afraid someone will find them. The day before the fox-hunt we got the shark-meat and dragged it around——"

"You told us about the shark-meat," said Séamus suddenly. "You knew about it then."

"Yes, I knew about it. The shark-meat worked well. The day of the hunt, I was afraid you would be going to the foxes. That's why I wouldn't let you out of school."

"That was why!"

"Someone would surely have seen you. When I found the foxes, I guessed Patsy was mixed up in it, because when he wrote his story it was all about foxes. Can we go there now?"

"Yes, yes. Have you seen the cubs?"

"Only through the crack by the door."

Mr. Thornton was well able to walk along the top of the wall. It was a clear, sunny afternoon with a west wind blowing steadily, still cold with the remains of winter. Down in the field where the foxes were, it was sheltered so that it felt like summer. In the last few days the brambles had turned green and the ferns had begun to shoot again, curled and wrinkled like clothes that have been put away for the winter.

They opened the door and led the big foxes out. The

cubs tumbled and played all around them. That was a moment of intense joy, when they saw Mr. Thornton's astonishment and pleasure.

He knelt down, and immediately the cubs came and nipped at him, growling and yapping with excitement.

"Look at their ears—their tails—their eyes!" Mr. Thornton did not know which to admire first. "They're so healthy, they're a credit to you all. You provided them with everything they could possibly want."

"But they're not safe," said Patsy. "Some day they'll be found. If we're only rearing them to be killed at last, it would have been better not to have reared them at all."

"Could we bring them to my house?"

"What about Molly?"

"I couldn't hide them from Molly. I might be able to make her keep it secret."

"Maybe for a day or two," said Séamus, "but I doubt it. My mother says that Molly is the biggest gossip in Galway Bay."

"It's a good job I don't usually have secrets," Mr. Thornton said. "We can't leave someone with them all the time. That would be noticed quicker than anything. One thing I can do is to give you food and milk for them. That should lessen the chances of people finding them."

It was an immense relief not to have to collect th foxes' food. The boys all found that they had got such a habit of slipping pieces of food into their pockets that they could hardly stop themselves now that there was no more need for it. Even their way of looking at cows had changed. Instead of admiring their shining skins or their calm, quiet behaviour, they saw only whether there was a big bag of milk from which a little would not be missed.

"I'm glad not to have to collect soda-bread any more," Patsy said. "We must have got the name of being the four hungriest boys on the island."

"Or the four most curious," said Michael. "I'm sure some people thought we were coming around to pick up the gossip."

"That's nothing to what they'll think if they find the foxes," said Patsy.

Now they were all expected to eat the foxes' rations at meals as well as their own. Patsy's mother said, after a day or two:

"You're losing your fine appetite again, a mac. I thought there for a while that you were going to grow as big as Finn MacCool, with the amount of food that was going into you, though you didn't have much of the signs of it on you, I must say."

She looked him over doubtfully. Patsy promised himself there and then that he would tell her all about the foxes some day, even if he had to wait until he was grown up. He knew she would enjoy them, if they could be shown to her. She had the name of rearing the best sheep-dog pups on the island, so that people often brought her a delicate litter to keep for them for a few weeks, until they were settled in their health. It was not that she gave them different food from the usual. She seemed to be able to give them some of her own goodness, in the way that she talked to them and played with them, so that they became happy and contented.

"And the world knows that a contented child is a healthy one," she said sometimes. "It's the same with pups, for sure."

Now, every morning the boys went to Mr. Thornton's

house at eight o'clock and they all carried the food to the foxes. Mr. Thornton always prepared it the evening before, so that Molly would not find the potato pot warm when she came. He had found an old pot-oven in his shed, and this made a fine feeding-trough. Every morning, they looked over towards Galway, watching for the boat that would take the foxes away, and every morning, though they longed for it to come, they were glad when it was not there.

"There's five of us to fight for those foxes," Mr. Thornton said one morning a week later.

Patsy said nothing. Every time they came to the shelter now he was afraid they would find that the foxes were dead. It would be easy to fight for them, compared with this. Someone might find them by accident and just kill them all at once without waiting to think or to call anyone. Patsy was filled with horror at this idea. He knew that it was possible, so much were foxes hated and feared for their evil powers.

But it was their reputation for evil powers that saved them in the end. Patsy never forgot how they learned what had happened.

The boys were sitting on their usual bench in Patsy's kitchen. Mr. Thornton was on the right-hand hob, in the place of honour. Seán Mór had his big chair with the arms, by the kitchen table, partly turned towards the door so that he could greet the visitors one by one as they came in. There was a fine fire, and though the summer was on its way, it was cold enough still for everyone to enjoy the glow of the burning turf. Seán the Post was there, and his wife Kate, who had skipped quickly into the hob opposite Mr. Thornton although she knew well that this place belonged by right to the woman of the house. Patsy glared at her until his mother laid her hand on his knee and said:

"I'll sit with you this evening, agrá. That way I'll be near the turf-stack for mending the fire."

It was this kind of politeness that had earned her the reputation of being the most hospitable woman on the island.

Kate hunched forward with her elbows on her knees and her bare toes scrabbling in the warm turf ashes.

"Tell me now, Nellie, how are the chookies with you?" she asked eagerly.

"Only one glugger," said Nellie. "They hatched out this morning, God bless them. 'Tis grand weather for them. How are they with you?"

"Pulling and hauling," said Kate mournfully, though Patsy knew that she had no less than five clutches of chickens hatched out in the last week.

Kate always had the poor mouth, he thought, for fear that she might be expected to give away something if she looked too prosperous. Her husband Seán spoiled it all for her by his pride in his wife's housekeeping.

"I'll say for her what she can't say for herself, for fear she'd be boasting," he said now. "The shed is walking with chickens, the finest in Connaught. There's no one like herself to rear them. There's three months' eating on them, and it's yourself will get the first of them, Nellie, for you're always a good friend. Isn't that right, Kate?"

"It is, faith," said Kate, but it was easy to see that she was in agonies at the idea of having to give away even one of her great flock of chickens.

While Seán the Post was speaking, there was a commotion at the door. Mike Hernon and Peter, Colm's father, pushed their chairs aside, the legs grating noisily on the floor. The other visitors stood up and lifted their creepie stools out of the way, so that the middle of the floor was left clear for the new arrival.

It was an old, old man. He was so bent at the knees that he looked as if he were in the act of stooping. His back was curved over like a thorn bush that has been blown all its life long by the Atlantic winds. His white hair was so thick that it seemed to lift his old battered hat right off his head. The hat was a greenish grey with age and the brim flopped here and there so that his face was partly covered. He had no beard, though his neighbours often wondered how he managed to shave without cutting his head off, at his age. The part of his face that showed under his hat was weatherbeaten until it looked like old leather. He wore an aged báinín over three or four woollen jerseys which were riddled with holes.

Nellie Seán Mór sprang up and said heartily:

"Morty! You're welcome, indeed, though I never thought to see you out visiting again. You're a sight for sore eyes, so you are. Kate, let you sit here on the bench with the boys and let Morty in on the hob."

Kate had to move, though it was something for her vanity that she was given Nellie's own place. Seán Mór welcomed Morty too, and led him in and placed him on the hob as if he were handling a basket of eggs.

"Morty Quinn!" Séamus said softly into Patsy's ear. "How did he get this far? He hasn't even been to the Chapel for years and years——"

They could not discuss him with all the company so close. Patsy had always heard that Morty could walk only a few steps, because of his great age. Several times, when he had been near the house, he had heard the old man rustling about as you might hear rats rustling in a stack of barley. Only once he had glimpsed him in the distance, a slow, grey patch moving against the grey wall of his house.

When he was settled on the hob, Morty panted for breath, leaning on the knob of his stick. Patsy saw that Mr. Thornton was watching him sharply. Morty spoke in a high, quavering voice, moving his head up and down as if this helped him to get the words out.

"I never thought I'd go visiting again either, Nellie, and when I do there's no house I'd rather go to than your own. You were a fine, warm-hearted girl always. Ay, you were, for sure. And signs on you with the grand fire you have. A good fire is the finest thing of all."

" 'Tis so, 'tis so," said Seán Mór.

No one else spoke. Respect for Morty's great age kept them silent, but also they were anxious to hear what brought him so far, after all the years. Morty knew well that they were curious. He lifted his chin and his eyes glittered maliciously in the fire-light.

"Ye were talking of chickens and I coming in the door," he said slyly.

"We were, faith," said Seán the Post. " 'Tis the time of year for them."

"You have them in plenty?"

"Ay, thanks to my wife."

"You're in luck, so, for you'll be able to ransom yourself and your wife in the times to come."

"Ransom? What is this? What is he talking about?"

Morty stopped the questions with a thump of his stick on the hearth.

"There's a black time in store for us all. Often I heard my grandfather say it, that it would be a black day for us when the foxes would start living in houses like Christians, instead of as they always did, in holes in the ground."

"What nonsense is this?" said Seán Mór, startled out of his good manners for a moment.

Morty thumped again, this time with temper.

"Nonsense, you call it! The old people had wisdom, and 'tis well to respect it. This very day I saw a sight that I wouldn't have believed in if someone told it to me. We always heard it said that foxes are able to change themselves into people. My grandfather, God rest his soul, he had many a story about them. Once he told me how a decent, quiet man married a girl from some out-of-the-way part of Connemara. She had no relations living, she said. He met her at the May fair in Galway and he should have had better sense than to be taking up with a girl that couldn't show as much as a cousin to prove where she came from. Well, time passed, and she was nice in the house, baking and mending his shirts and doing all the things that a good wife ought to do. And then one day she says to him: 'I'll be going, Pat, 'tis too closed in for me, in this place.' And with that didn't she turn into a fox and go running out the door. He was ashamed for a long time to tell the people what happened her, the poor man. But in the end he had to tell, for they all noticed that she was gone."

"Those are only old stories," said Seán the Post.

"Wait, just wait till I tell my story, and you'll change your tune," Morty squeaked with excitement. "My land is full of brambles and briars, as ye all know well. I'm doing no more work on the land, only waiting for God to call me. Today, after dinner, I took a notion to walk the land, as well as I'd be able, and I went down to a little small field that I have, over the sea, with a wall around it. I used to keep sheep in it long ago, and there's a kind of a hut there that I built for them, to keep the weather off them in the winter-time.

"When I got to the field, I knew there was something strange at once. The grass was all flattened, and some of the old ferns were cut. 'Take it easy, now,' said I to myself. I went over to the hut like you'd creep on a bird, and I looked in through a crack, and what did I see?"

He looked around at the company, his chin stuck in the air. No one spoke, though everyone was leaning forward eagerly.

"What did I see but a family of black foxes, and they living inside in my hut as comfortably as I live in my own house!"

"God look down on us!"

"That's what I saw." Morty was clearly pleased with the effect he had produced. "They had everything a fox would need—ferns to lie on, and the floor clean and dry the way you'd know they had swept it. Didn't they even have a pot-oven by the door to eat out of! And the best of all was that they had turned the course of the stream to send it through the field, the way they'd have water to drink. I'm telling you, 'tis a black day for us all. They'll do harm to Inishownan. Soon they'll be coming around to the houses, demanding the best of everything. Them that can pay them off with chickens will be safe enough, but what is to happen to the widow and the orphan, and the old and feeble like myself? Sorry I am that I lived to see this day!"

He said the last words in such a heavy tone that Kate Seán the Post gave a wail of terror. Old Morty looked at her with satisfaction. Nellie said briskly:

"Those are only stories. Sure, the world knows a fox is only an animal, like a dog or a cat or a goat——"

"Take care! Take care! They have the power of making themselves unseen too, and coming and listening in the houses to what the people are saying about them!"

" 'Tis bad manners of them, then," said Nellie, still trying to joke the old man out of his prophecies of disaster.

Morty stood up, white and trembling with fury.

"I'll say no more," he said in a terrible voice. "I'll go home to my house to-night and I'll bar the doors. And tomorrow I'll meet any man that comes, and bring him to see what I've seen. Then we'll know who is telling the truth."

He walked totteringly towards the door, opened it and went out. In the silence they could hear his stick thumping on the road, growing fainter and fainter until it died away altogether.

10

Seán Mór was the first to move.

"The old people were a fright for those stories," he said with a laugh. "Old Morty is gone queer in the head in the latter end of his days. Foxes living like Christians in a house! And black foxes, at that. Sure, the world knows that foxes are red."

The company relaxed and Patsy heard several people murmur words of pity for old Morty. Then Mr. Thornton spoke for the first time:

"They're not exactly black. They're called silver foxes, because there are white hairs through the black ones."

"That may be in other parts of the world," said Seán Mór, "but I have never heard of a black or silver fox on this island."

"Except the ones that Morty saw," said Mr. Thornton gently.

"Surely you don't believe that ráiméis? That foxes would live in a house?"

" 'Tis true, all the same."

Patsy said:

"You're not going to tell!"

"We must tell now," Mr. Thornton said gently. "Do

you think that Morty won't tell everyone on the island? I was afraid that this would happen."

"What are you talking about?" Seán Mór demanded. "Speak plain, man! Is Morty's story true?"

Every head was bent forward, every eye was fixed on Mr. Thornton as he answered:

"Yes, it is true that there is a family of foxes in his shed, but it is not true that they are looking after themselves. Myself and the boys, there, are doing that."

Still the men could not understand it. Mr. Thornton explained patiently. At last they began to believe him, and then such an argument started that it looked like lasting the whole night through. All foxes were evil, the men said, and they must be killed. Mr. Thornton pointed out that they were not red, chicken-stealing foxes, but a superior kind. Besides, they belonged to a man in Dublin who would be coming for them any day now. Probably he was a fox in disguise, the men said. If he were allowed to land, he might change into a fox and run off to hide in a burrow on Inishownan, only coming out at night to raid the hen-houses. At this Mr. Thornton got angry and threatened to bring out the Archbishop from his palace in Tuam, to pray over them the way you would pray over a heathen. He was no heathen, Seán Mór protested, but after a life-time of hearing that foxes were villains, it was hard to expect him to take them to his bosom.

"Not to your bosom, exactly," said Mr. Thornton. "Just leave them alone until their owner comes."

"But the villainy and devilment that they'll be up to in the meantime—what about that?"

Mr. Thornton guaranteed that the foxes would do no harm, but Seán the Post said:

"No one can guarantee that a fox won't do harm. If you were an islandman you'd know that. I only ever heard one way with foxes and that was to polish them off every chance you get."

"It's not that we believe every word of those old stories," said Peter, who had been very silent until now. "But it's hard to go against what you were taught and you in petticoats. Now, 'tis true that you are a man of knowledge but you're not an islandman, and sure, no one can know everything."

"It's this way," said Seán Mór. "If we kill the foxes, we'll have peace of mind. If we don't, there's not one of us will sleep easy, but fearing all the time that those lads will be coming to make off with his wife or his children, not to mind the stock of his land."

Suddenly Patsy was out in the middle of the floor. He never knew how he got there. If he had taken time to think, it's certain that he would never have faced all the men with such courage. His voice sounded sharp and fierce, like a terrier yapping among sheepdogs.

"You'll kill them," he said. "Who is going to do it? Who is going to walk into the shelter where the foxes are, and kill the six of them one after the other? From what you're saying, they're powerful lads, are foxes. The first man that touches one of those foxes may find himself turned into a goat or some other animal that's worse, a pig maybe. When I see who has the courage to go in first and kill one of those foxes, I'll say to myself: 'That's the bravest man on Inishownan.' "

Mr. Thornton sat back into the chimney corner, as far as he could go. In the dim light of the fire, Patsy could see him smile to himself for a second. Then he looked serious again.

There was a long silence. Patsy still stood there with his fists clenched, feeling more and more every minute the awfulness of what he had done. For a boy to take such a part in the men's conversation was a terrible thing. But they did not look angry. He could hardly see their faces because their eyes were turned down to the floor. No one seemed to want to look at him, not even his father, Seán Mór.

Then gradually he began to understand why. They were afraid, every man of them. Not one of them had the courage to undertake to kill those strange, powerful foxes, lest the man who did it, and his family, should suffer some terrible misfortune. Patsy thought of the soft, furry cubs, of their big ears and short bushy tails, of their silky tongues that licked your hand so gently. He thought of the mother fox who leaned against you as if she were trying to show her gratitude, and of the father fox who licked the cubs all over every evening, so that they went to bed clean. How could anyone think them evil? He would not say this, of course. All the better, if they had such a reputation. Perhaps it would save their lives now.

And this was what happened. Seán Mór said at last:

"That man will come in a day or three, I suppose. 'Tis long since ye wrote to him."

He came the very next afternoon, on the Post Boat. He hardly had his foot on the quay when Mr. Thornton was asking him:

"What kept you so long? We thought you would never come."

"Jaundice," said the man. "I turned as yellow as a kite's

claw. The doctor wouldn't let me out. How are my foxes? I brought a cage to put them in."

Kate had come down with Seán the Post to meet the boat. Patsy thought it was well that the man had come on the Post Boat, because in this way he had escaped some notice. Everyone had expected him to come on a boat of his own, hired in Galway. They would have seen the strange boat miles away and would have been down in their hundreds to watch it land. Now Kate said to Willie:

"And are you going to bring a cageful of foxes into Galway on your boat? Aren't you afraid they'll make a wreck of it on you?"

"I have my instructions," said Willie. "That's the kind of risk you take when you enter the service of the Government. Your husband would tell you that."

While the cage was being put ashore, Patsy ran home for his donkey and cart. They loaded the cage and the mail-bags and started up the hill. They stopped at the Post Office to take off the mail-bags. Kate trotted in quickly to be there before them. As they went on, Mr. Thornton and the fox man walked ahead. The boys could hear them talking like old friends. Séamus said:

"I don't mind handing over our foxes to that man. He'll know how to look after them."

"It's going to be lonesome without them," said Patsy.

They had to leave the cart at Mr. Thornton's house, with the donkey tied to the post by the door. Then they all walked along the top of the wall and came down into the field where the shelter was.

"Four cubs," said the fox man, "and in fine condition. You boys can take one each and go out in front. Then the parents will be more anxious to follow."

He handed the biggest cub to Colm, and one each to the others. Then he and Mr. Thornton took up the two big foxes, and they started in procession back to Mr. Thornton's house.

After having seen the foxes living free in their own house, it hurt Patsy to see them bundled into the cage. They sat on their hunkers, like dogs, looking out through the bars with their ears cocked forward. Patsy asked:

"Will they spend the rest of their lives in a cage like that?"

"Certainly not," said the fox man. "You'd better all come and see them when they are established in the Dublin zoo. Their living quarters are rather like what you gave them. There's a little house at the back, and a garden in front with a stream and a pool. There are bars of course, to keep the people who visit the zoo from coming too near. They won't be shut in at all."

This was great news.

"I'd like to see them again," said Patsy. "But Dublin is a long way off."

"It's not as far as you think. Mr. Thornton will come too. He has promised."

They untied the donkey and started back towards the Post Office, where they found Willie sitting at the table enjoying a big dish of potatoes and salty bacon.

"Come in, come in," said Willie, as if the house were his. "I never like to eat alone. There's enough here for all. Isn't that right, ma'am?"

So Kate had to invite the fox man and Mr. Thornton to dinner. She stared at the boys with narrowed eyes, wishing them to go home, but Séamus said:

"We'll just stay here, with the foxes. We can eat at home later on."

"Thanks, all the same," said Michael, though Kate had offered them nothing.

Seán the Post was slowly going over the mail, which he had spread out on the Post Office table. When the men were seated and about to begin their meal, he said:

"A letter for you, Master Thornton."

Kate took it from him quickly.

"A letter that's printed, from Dublin. Open it up, Master. We'll take no notice of you," she said.

She stood in front of him with her lips parted and her hands on her hips, almost holding her breath in her eagerness to know what could be in such an important-looking letter.

Mr. Thornton slit the envelope open with his knife.

"Look at that," said Kate admiringly. "He does it so neatly, you'd think he was gutting a fish."

After a quick glance at the letter, Mr. Thornton said:

"Patsy has won the competition for a story. It was an all-Ireland competition," he explained to the fox man. "It's a great honour to win it, for Inishownan."

"It is indeed. What was your story about?"

Patsy was so surprised that his voice came in a hoarse whisper.

"It was about a fox-hunt," he said.

Immediately the fox man looked offended, but Mr. Thornton explained quickly:

"Patsy was on the side of the fox. Tell him the story, Patsy."

So Patsy told the story while they ate. At the end the fox man said:

"That was a good story. That deserved to win."

While they were in the Post Office, a crowd had gathered around the cart outside. The people were looking curiously in at the foxes, and they were rather silent. Mr. Thornton stood in the Post Office doorway and said:

"It seems to me they brought good luck to Inishownan instead of bad. Here's Patsy has won the competition for a story. And Patrick O'Flaherty died in America and left his millions to be divided out among you. There's not much bad luck in that."

" 'Tis true, 'tis true, indeed," the people said.

Michael remembered how the Post Boat had almost crushed Séamus in the currach, but he did not say it aloud. That had surely been good luck too. Old Jamesy Lynch said:

"There's good luck and good luck. Sometimes what looks like good luck is not healthy at all."

But no one took any notice of Jamesy because they knew that he was one of the very few people on the island who had not the smallest drop of O'Flaherty blood in them. Until the news of the legacy had come, indeed, he had been accustomed to boast of this, and to say that the O'Flahertys were a wild, fierce tribe. He used to remind people of the old prayer that used to be said in certain families that were enemies of the tribe: 'From the ferocious O'Flahertys, Oh Lord, deliver us.' Remembering this put the people into good humour now, and they began to say that it was possible that black foxes would bring good luck, while the red kind might still be dangerous. Besides, they could not help admiring the lively cubs and their sleek, healthy-looking parents.

124

Everyone came down to the quay to watch the foxes leave the island. They were very respectful, and Patsy noticed that they were careful not to say anything against foxes in their hearing. Mike stowed the cage on deck between the mail-bags.

"I thought you said we were to bring back a load of foxes. Sure, anyone can see that them are dogs," he said.

And he spat into the sea with contempt for the ignorance of people.

It was a calm, clear day, and the sea shone like pale blue silk. The high hills of Clare were a darker blue, veined with silver. The Post Boat sailed off as smoothly as a swan taking to the water. The boys stood with Mr. Thornton and watched it until it was no more than a little black speck, like a fly on a window-pane. Mr. Thornton turned away and said:

"They'll have a calm passage the whole way. It's just as well. The big foxes might have remembered the storm if it had been rough today." Suddenly he burst out laughing. "Wasn't it strange that no one asked that man what his name was?"

"I thought of it," said Patsy, "but I thought it might not be polite to ask directly."

"It would have been quite polite," said Mr. Thornton, "but it's just as well you didn't. I asked him, on the way to my house. He said his name is Fox—John Fox. If the men had heard that, they would never have believed that he was not a fox in disguise."

" 'Tis a queer chance," said Michael doubtfully.

"Not such a chance," said Mr. Thornton. "He told me that his name being Fox got him interested in foxes when he was a boy. When he grew up and became a biologist, he became a specialist in foxes. Now he knows the different forms of the breed throughout the world."

"And is he paid to be a specialist in foxes?"

Colm was pulling at Patsy's sleeve and whispering:

"Patsy! The fourpence! We forgot the fourpence for the stamp."

Patsy thought about that for a moment. Then he said:

"We'll get it from him when we go to see him in Dublin."

Mr. Thornton was answering his last question:

"Yes. He's paid by a body of people who do research in natural history."

Patsy only barely knew what this meant. It seemed to mean that there were people in the world who spent their whole lives in doing what he and Séamus and Michael and Colm had just done for the black foxes. After a moment he said to Mr. Thornton:

"Could I do that sort of work when I grow up?"

"You'd have to leave the island to study."

"I could come back sometimes."

"Yes, you could come back."

"Will you help me?"

"Yes, I will always help you," said Mr. Thornton.